1/22

THE LEGEND OF THE DREAM GIANTS

THE LEGEND OF THE
DREAM GIANTS

WRITTEN AND ILLUSTRATED BY

DUSTIN HANSEN

SHADOW
MOUNTAIN

For my eleven-year-old self,
who needed this book then as much as I need it now.
Perhaps even more.

Text and illustrations © 2022 Dustin Hansen

Visit us at shadowmountain.com

Library of Congress Cataloging-in-Publication Data
(CIP data on file)
ISBN 978-1-62972-986-2

Printed in China   10/2021
RR Donnelley, Dongguan, China

10   9   8   7   6   5   4   3   2   1

A thousand-thousand
nights ago . . .

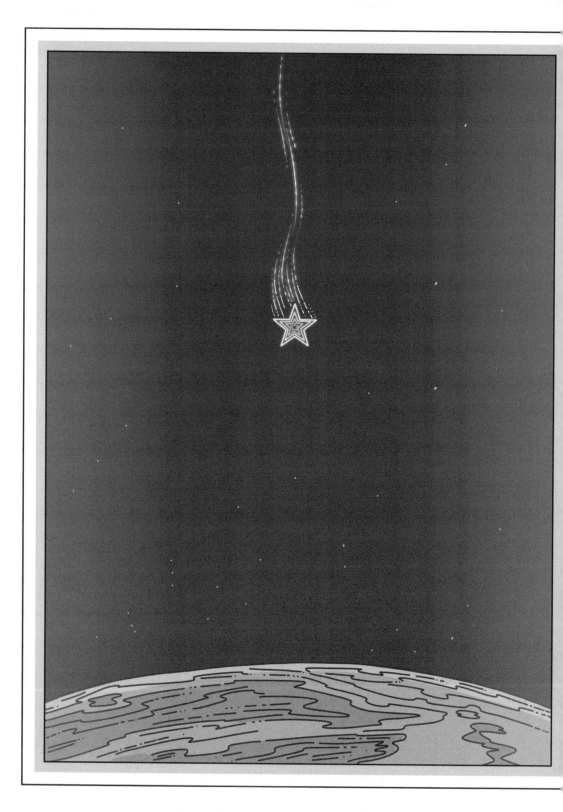

BOOK ONE

WHERE WE LEARN
OF GIANTS,
OLD AND YOUNG

WHILE THE CITY SLEEPS

The giant woke beneath Old-Oak, wild hair and branches mingling, the ground beneath his bottom crisp with autumn leaves. He stood and waited as patient as moss for the townsfolk to disappear behind closed doors, then went to his tiptoes to peek above the branches. The town was asleep. His eyes told him so, but it was his stomach that urged him to leave his hiding spot.

No, *urged* was not the word. A giant's hunger doesn't urge. A giant's hunger commands.

He crept to a stone-covered road, where he picked up his pace. Watchful-moon above and street-mice below his only companions.

A leather satchel hung from his shoulder, a bag with crude stitches of once-red thread, now faded to the color of mud. His wide hand dropped to the bottom of the satchel, and he delicately touched the treasures he had brought along for trade.

The aroma of roasting meat called to Berg, and he followed his nose to a little home at the edge of sleeping-city. He went to his hands and knees to look eye to eye with the little window, then he coaxed it open with a chipped and muddy fingernail.

The window moaned a warning to the sleeping people inside, but Berg knew the window's cry was a game it must play. It had mocked him in the past, but it always let him in.

Crouching like a stone, a large and silent stone, he waited for his eyes to adjust to the dark inside the little house. It was an inky-black space, a playground for crickets and other night-bugs. Berg could read the slightest cues, the simplest silhouettes, the most subtle hints in the near-dark. A life in the woods had earned him this. He drew a breath through his wide nose, filling his chest with the fatty aroma of the roast.

The slab of meat hung from a chain above a pile of glowing coals. The giant licked his lips, then reached through the window. The back of his hand brushed against the ceiling as he stretched toward the feast. He threaded the roast from the hook above the coals, then carefully slipped the meal from the house with something that almost resembled grace.

The moon reflected off the marbled surface of the meat, and the young giant's stomach commanded him to take a bite, but Berg ignored his stomach and tucked his new prize inside his bag. He knew he'd enjoy the meal more if he could eat in peace. Standing in the middle of the street offered no peace, for the people of sleeping-city were unfriendly toward Berg.

No, *unfriendly* was not the word. They hated him. Although it was not his fault, the people hated Berg and feared him greatly.

Berg dipped into his bag, tumbling his greasy fingers beneath the stolen roast to pull out a handful of forest-jewels. He sifted through his fine possessions in search of the perfect trade. He found a river-polished rock with a vein of sparkling silver slicing through like a streak of lightning. He remembered finding the stone in the bottom of a river. The rock was full of memories, for he had carried lightning-stripe-stone for nearly three years. Ever since she had gone. Ever since Berg had been alone.

To Berg the giant-boy, the lightning-stripe-stone contained great worth. But the roast was large and smelled of fire, and he knew the stone was the price he should pay.

He placed lightning-stripe-stone on the windowsill and pushed the window closed, leaving behind a smudge on the glass. A ribbon of moonlight touched the stone as it waited to be discovered. Berg knew he'd paid too much, but he loved to overpay for the food he found, so he walked away without regret.

In the center of town, Berg found a garden patch behind a small cottage. He dug in the soil with his colossal hands, uncovering a few dozen potatoes hiding beneath the earth. With his satchel nearly full, the young giant went to the front door of the cottage and left behind more forest-jewels—three bird skulls and a sky-blue egg, once again overpaying for the food he'd taken.

He dusted off his hands as he continued his search through town, cutting through a small park bordered by a freshly painted fence. The heady smell of fresh paint wafted through the air. The white fence glowed blue in the moonlight, which made Berg smile. But then he happened upon a crude painting in the center of the fence. Sloppily painted by an angry hand was the image of a giant. As he studied the image, his stomach rolled like an avalanche: tumbly and heavy and cold.

The painted giant held a club above his wild hair, and his mouth gaped to reveal a deadly row of sharp teeth. Townsfolk with pitchforks and torches and pointed-sticks surrounded the giant. Written in bold letters above the hurtful portrait was a single word: Ünhold!

Berg had seen and heard the word before. It was one of the few words the giant could read. It was a word wrongly used to describe him, for he was not Ünhold, the storied giant who once roamed the earth and frightened old and young alike. Berg knew Ünhold was an ugly word full of venom and fear. Every bit as ugly as the painting on the fence.

The young giant's shoulders drooped as he faced the painting. He dipped into his satchel, digging beneath the raw potatoes and the roast meat.

One by one, Berg removed the forest-jewels, the rocks and bones and feathers and the shells of river-snails. He lined the treasures along the top row of the fence. One jewel per slat until his hands were bare. It would take him a month to replace his goods, but he hoped the people of sleeping-city would find the offering and know it was from him. That they would learn that he was good. That he was not Ünhold the Giant.

He hoped they would see that he was kind.

He left the park and hurried to the opposite end of town from Old-Oak and its carpet of crunchy leaves. He didn't stop to look for food, for he had nothing left to trade. Besides, Berg wanted to leave. He needed to return to the forest, for unlike the city filled with those who would harm him for things he had not done, the forest was a place to rest. The forest was good.

A dark figure perched next to the last house in town, hiding like a raven in the night. A bony old woman buried beneath a crocheted shawl scowled up at Berg as he approached. He was easily five times her height and fifty times her weight, but the sight of the old woman worried the young giant. He looked at her, staring into her black-jewel eyes, doing his best to let her know he meant no harm.

The old woman aimed a crooked finger his way and growled through a toothless mouth. She mumbled something, then spat, her cottony spittle landing upon his foot.

"Ünhold," she said in a voice as thin as paper and rough as bark.

Berg turned and rushed away, knowing what was coming next.

The old woman spoke louder. "Ünhold!"

Berg ran, his bag heavy with food, his mind weighed down with sorrow.

"Ünhold!" she cawed.

Berg ran with all his might, his feet pounding the earth as he fled toward the deep-wild-woods. He knew the people of sleeping-city would soon follow with their pitchforks and torches and pointed-sticks.

Berg cried as he ran, not because he was afraid of the people, but because the people were afraid of him.

AMONG TALL PINES

The forest was familiar to Berg in the most personal of ways. He'd spent his life among tall pines. He held a kinship with the ancient trees—their trunks sturdy and immoveable, their tough skin coarse and cracked like his, their skyward tops towering above him. He loved the forest, for it made him feel small.

Berg carved a winding path between the trees. He'd not stopped moving since he'd run from the sleeping-city. He chugged on through the night, past his old forest home and on to find another. A fresh start away from those with pitchforks and pointed-sticks. He was tired, but the cool earth felt nice beneath his callused feet, as thick and dark as elephant hide.

He had devoured the raw potatoes and smoked roast as he'd traveled. He wished he could have made his meal last longer. He'd added bulbous toadstools, a few unripe berries, and two bird eggs to his satchel along the way. Spending a life among the pines taught Berg that the forest provided tasty treats to those hungry enough to look.

Thunderclouds hid the sky, hanging so low Berg wondered if the trees would claw them open. The sun had set behind the clouds, but a bit of light remained as the sky began to weep.

He crouched below the lower branches of an ancient tree and searched in the near-dark for a dry spot to make his bed. Berg ambled forward, bent over to keep his massive head beneath the low, swooping arms of the primordial trees. He found a fallen log as large as a house that had lost its fight with time. A ball of unearthed roots and two large branches gouged the earth, propping the fallen tree high enough off the ground to offer shelter to the young giant.

He scooped up armloads of dry pine needles and crinkly leaves from the floor of the deep-wild-woods and made a soft bed beneath his fallen-tree-home. It was tighter than he'd hoped inside the space.

With barely enough room to wiggle, Berg nestled in, then opened his satchel to find a single mushroom and the two eggs. He swallowed them whole, eggshells and all, as he watched a storm swell around him. The wind and rain were familiar, lonely sounds that made Berg feel sad. He loved his deep-wild-woods, but he would give them up without remorse if he could live among the people of sleeping-city.

He knew it was foolish, but he closed his eyes and wished all the same. He wished they weren't so scared, but they were no different than those from other cities Berg had known.

Hiding beneath bridges and behind barns, he'd heard their awful tales of Ünhold the Giant who walked the earth smelling of rot and ruin. Stealing everything from silver spoons to children.

It was unfair. Berg had not asked to be a giant, he simply was. He didn't smell of rot and ruin. Berg had no need for spoons, and he would never steal a child. Why, he was nothing but a child himself.

He was just big. Big and all alone.

Berg cried as the storm matured around him. He lay silent beneath his fallen-tree-home. The rain washed dust from the air and awakened the smells of the forest. He breathed in deep, pulling the timberland inside his lungs, tasting the cool, forest-spiced air in his nose and mouth.

The autumn air was cold, but it had little effect on Berg's thick hide. With his wide shoulders scraping against the inside of his fallen-tree-home, he inched the remaining food from his satchel and buried it beneath his pine-needle bed. The empty satchel became a makeshift pillow for the young giant's head.

He lay in silence within his hole and listened to the sounds of his deep-wild-woods. Owls hooted and night-frogs chirped, energized by the little drencher. A raccoon chattered nearby, and the trees swooshed and creaked a forest lullaby as they swayed back and forth with the wind.

Berg's eyelids grew heavy. He blinked, feeling the grit and grime from his journey scrub against his tired eyes. Sleep grabbed him in her arms and pulled down slowly, holding him against the earth within her embrace. He was nearly asleep when the sounds of the forest hushed.

He peeked out of his fallen-tree-home, searching for a glimpse of watchful-moon, and he thought he saw the figure of a man. He looked to the sky again, silently asking the moon to show herself and offer him a better view. Perhaps what he had seen was merely a pile of rocks.

With his eyes wide, Berg tilted his head forward until his heavy brow pressed against the rough hide of the fallen log. He slowed his breath to a glacier's pace, not wanting to catch the attention of the dark shape in the woods. Curiosity and fear swirled inside Berg's near-empty stomach. Rain leaked into his fallen-tree-home, and Berg focused on the water around him as he tried to blend into the earth.

Watchful-moon blew away a cloud and shined down into the forest. She lent Berg her eyes, casting a faint outline upon the figure. With the hints the moon provided, Berg could no longer tell himself the silhouette before him was a pile of rocks. The figure was much larger than Berg was, easily twenty feet tall and as wide and sturdy as a barn.

Lightning struck as the young giant studied the massive creature, and the bright flash momentarily robbed Berg's vision. He blinked his eyes shut, feeling mud and rainwater seep into the cracks and crevices of his face as he furrowed his brow and tightened his mouth. When he opened his eyes, the beast had gone.

It took an hour, perhaps two, for the little giant to wash the image of the beast out of his mind's eye. Eventually the storm cleared, and watchful-moon washed the forest around him with her light.

Without knowing it had had happened, Berg's thick eyelids grew too heavy for him to hold. He slipped into sleep, leaving behind the image of the figure in the forest and the hurtful drawing on the fence.

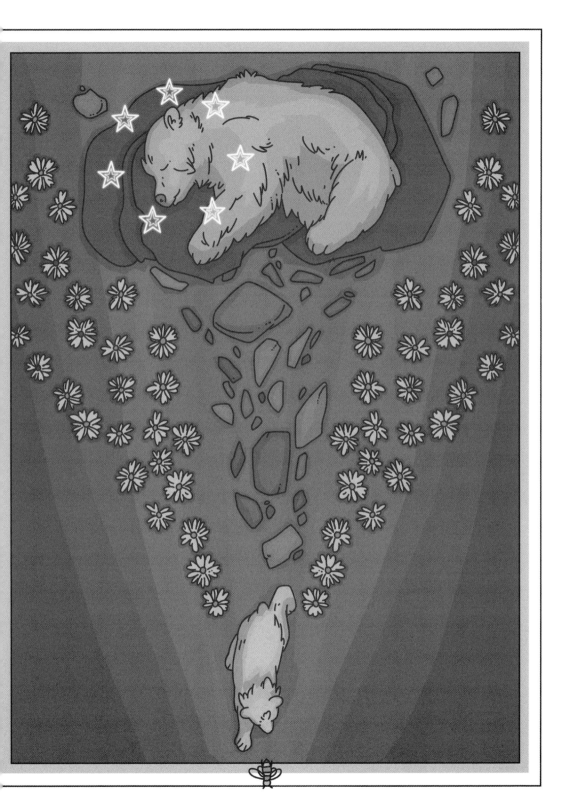

A SCAR IN THE WOODS

The dream jolted Berg awake as it had done a hundred-hundred nights before. He did not like the dream, but whenever he walked the deep-wild-woods alone, the dream seemed to follow him no matter how hard he tried to leave it behind.

Rain had visited the forest throughout the night, stirring but not waking the young giant as he slept beneath his fallen-tree-home. He finished off the mushrooms and a few unripe berries for breakfast, but the forest foods only teased his hunger.

He crawled from his resting spot and followed his ears to a nearby stream, where he drank until his stomach sloshed with icy water. Sitting on a flat rock, he dipped his toes in the little brook as he watched fat, green-backed trout dine on scuds and larvae. He tried to catch the fish, but it was a foolish game for one with such large hands and arms as thick as trees. As he watched the fish return to tease him, he smelled something tempting in the air: the sweet smoke of a cooking fire.

He looked in the direction of the smoke, sniffing and smiling as he detected hints of bacon grease and roasted onions. Nearby, a narrow trail revealed itself in the deep-wild-woods, leading toward the smoke. He left the little creek behind and followed the trail. The smell of smoke grew with every step, until he found a clearing in the woods, the trees stopping abruptly in a straight scar only a man could carve.

Berg hid behind the line of trees and watched as a family worked in groomed fields that surrounded a log cabin. A wisp of smoke drifted from a rock-lined chimney, and the large barn set behind the cabin somehow looked as old and natural as the forest it sat within.

A full garden spread out a few yards from Berg, row after neat row of green plants soaking up the sun between him and the cabin. He recognized the leafy greens of beets, the spiky shoots of onions, and the frilly tops of carrots, and his mouth began to water.

In the field behind the cabin, three sturdy men worked with their shirts off, their muscled backs shining with sweat. Before them, a matching pair of red mules yanked against powerful chains bound to a stubborn stump buried within the earth. The men shouted at the mule team, barking and howling like animals, prodding the team as they dug in the wet ground to coax the stump to leave its home. The mules pulled with all their might until the chain broke, sending a metal whip flying, nearly striking one of the suntanned ranchers.

Curses filled the air as the mules ran in perfect tandem into the forest, the sound of their hooves and the broken chain echoing long after the twin beasts had escaped view.

Berg was so transfixed by the working men and mules that he failed to notice the young child walking through the garden.

The boy was swinging a silver brush, bright and shining in the sun. A sliver of light flicked from the brush into Berg's eye. His mind spun, and his water-filled stomach seemed full of tiny fish, as he let himself wonder what it would be like to hold the brush himself.

No, *hold* was not the word. Berg did not want to simply hold the silver brush. Berg wanted to own it.

As the boy approached, Berg could hear him singing, happy and unaware that a giant was standing nearby. For a moment, the young giant let himself imagine that the boy and he could be friends. He wanted the silver brush; he'd never seen anything quite so beautiful in his entire life, but he'd gladly trade it to become friends with the boy in the garden.

Berg stood perfectly still as the boy skipped closer and closer to the trees. He held his breath and tried to think like a tree, a hopeful, friendly tree, until the child stopped directly below him.

The boy noticed the giant's feet first. The silver brush tumbled to the earth between the giant's bare toes as the boy slowly tilted his head up until he was looking into Berg's eyes.

The boy screamed, then ran back toward the cabin. "Papa! Papa! It's Ünhold, Papa! A troll!"

Berg was no troll, but he knew he couldn't stay. He glanced at the brush by his feet, then at the boy running through the garden, its high frills and spikes nearly up to the boy's waist. Berg ran back into the thick forest, leaving behind thoughts of carrots and beets, silver-brushes, and undiscovered friends.

ORANGE, WHITE, AND RED

Berg tried to sleep, but hunger seesawed with visions of the garden patch and the silver-brush, keeping him awake as near-dark became full-night. He waited until the crickets and night-frogs sang, telling the young giant the deep-wild-woods were safe.

By the light of watchful-moon, he retraced the path toward the family farm. The forest soil compressed beneath his bare feet, and soggy earth squished between his toes. The limbs of trees grabbed at Berg as he moved within them, stowaway leaves and pine needles clinging to his thick, black hair.

Berg found the clearing again, along with two sets of footprints: one set large and clumsy pressed deep into the earth, and one so small and graceful Berg could barely imagine how it must feel to run on feet so magical.

He went to his hands and knees and searched in the soft earth and grass for silver-brush, knowing that watchful-moon would help him find it, but the shiny object had disappeared. At first Berg was sad the brush was gone, but the more he thought about it, the more grateful he became.

Berg knew he would have taken the brush if he had found it. He also knew he'd be filled with guilt and reminded of the friend he could not have every time he looked at it.

Eventually Berg let his thoughts of the brush slip away as he focused on another task. A task of filling his belly.

Berg stood and looked into the clearing. Watchful-moon shone bright, out-lining the sharp pitch of the cabin roof against the dark sky. The forest seemed caught in a never-ending exhale as a cool night-breeze flowed over the garden.

He smiled as he watched the vegetables dance with the wind. The spiky tops of the onion plants quivered but stood strong. The fragile tendrils of the carrot patch seemed to move as one, shifting in unison like waves on a green ocean. The beet leaves were nearly black in the moonlight, but they seemed to be calling to Berg, motioning with their flat leaves for him to take them. To unearth them. To eat them.

He stood in the middle of the beets, but he couldn't remember having left the forest to join them. His hunger was powerful, demanding. He knelt, then carefully pinched one of the beet greens just above the soil. As he wiggled it back and forth, the giant felt the subtle tear of hairlike roots that surrounded the dark vegetable. He pulled the beet free, plucking it out like a loose tooth. After cleaning his reward upon his belly, he lifted it to his nose and breathed in the smell of soil and sweetness.

Berg tore the leafy greens from the beet, then popped the red root in his mouth. Earthy syrup covered his tongue and turned his teeth red as he smashed the dark-red-root between his molars. He added the greens next, chewing them and savoring how their bitter bite blended with the sugary beet.

He slipped his satchel from his shoulders and began to fill it with vegetables from the garden. He layered onions over a bed of beets, then topped it all with a few hundred carrots, lacy stems and all. He stood and shouldered his bag.

A raindrop tapped Berg on the shoulder, and he looked skyward just as watchful-moon slid behind an army of clouds. Berg overlooked the garden.

He'd harvested nearly a quarter of the family's food, and his satchel hung heavy against his shoulders. He had taken too much, and he had nothing to trade. He'd left all his forest-jewels in sleeping-city, lined upon the fence above the crude painting of the giant and the violent mob of angry men.

Berg didn't want to be a thief. Berg refused be a thief.

Rain tumbled down, tickling the top of his head and his wide shoulders. Lightning flashed again, startling him as he weighed his guilt in the rain. Thunder rumbled, and Berg trudged through the mud toward the cabin. He removed his satchel and emptied most of its contents upon the steps, lining the vegetables in neat rows of orange, white, and red.

Berg reshouldered his bag. It was lighter than before, but it still felt awkward upon his back. Then the shape of the stubborn stump caught his eye. He plowed through the muddy field, his feet sinking deep into the earth, covering the tiny tracks of the men and a hundred-hundred prints left behind by the hardworking mules.

Berg looked into the hole surrounding the stump. A broken shovel lay in the bottom. The wet-black earth in the pit contrasted with the white, scarred roots where the farmers had hacked with axes and saws. But the stump remained.

He climbed into the hole and found a root as wide as his forearm poking out from the side of the stump. He wrapped his hands around the root and lifted. The stump groaned and creaked. A few inches of play were all the stump was willing to give, and it thumped back into place with a mocking crack as Berg let up to catch his breath.

He took the root again. He pressed his face against the stump, feeling its rough bark. The boy-giant inhaled the ageless aroma of earth and pine sap. He pushed with his mighty legs until he heard the wood relent with a loud snap that echoed through the clearing, sounding like thunder. Berg lifted the stump out of the hole, upending it onto the soil above.

He stood straight, his head and shoulders rising from the hole like an enormous groundhog. Using the dismembered roots that remained behind as footholds, Berg unearthed himself.

He put his satchel over his shoulder for the third time that night, and if it weren't for the round bodies of the few beets left in the bottom of the sack, he would have sworn the pack was empty.

He'd overpaid once again, trading the removal of the stump for a half belly full of food. Rain rinsed clay from Berg as he tramped back through the forest toward his fallen-tree-home and a well-earned supper.

A ROARING RIVER

Berg belched, tasting the bitter bite of onions mixed with sweet beets and carrots. He didn't mind; in fact, he quite liked it. A fragrant reminder of his supper.

Perched on the bank of a little stream, Berg dipped his bulbous toes into the cool water. He watched the rolling brook as he daydreamed about returning to the small farm to collect more of the fall roots. But for that, he would need something more to trade.

The young giant knew he'd find forest-jewels at the bottom of the stream if he was patient enough. He loved the search itself, the sifting of rocks and stones smoothed by a hundred-hundred lifetimes of rolling water.

He plunged his hand into the stream and pulled out a handful of pebbles. He flicked them back into the water, one by one, as they failed to meet his high expectations. Only something truly special would do. Something valuable enough to trade for another load of produce.

He was considering a stone, white with swirls of pink and tawny yellow, when he heard men talking in the woods. Their gruff voices floated to him on the breeze.

"The beast slept here. Look," said a man, his voice quivering with fear.

"Quiet! It could be anywhere," said a second man, his voice pitched high and nearly boiling over with fright.

"Let it come. I'm ready," said a third voice, followed by the unmistakable sound of a gun being cocked.

"Don't be so sure," said the first man. "He went this way."

Berg dropped the remaining pebbles in his satchel to sort later, crossed the stream in a single stride, then worked his way into the cover of the deep-wild-woods. He tried to go quietly, but he knew he was only fooling himself. He was too big to stay hidden for long.

He heard the men shout. He couldn't make out what they said, but the frenzied pitch in their voices jolted Berg into a run. Forest-ferns and flowers crushed beneath his feet. He bowled over saplings and tore branches from the trees, leaving a tunnel behind him as wide as a cathedral.

A gunshot was fired. Then another. More shouting chased Berg through the timber.

By the time he saw the gray globe of the wasp nest, he barely had time to cover his face. Berg collided with the papery ghost, scattering wasps and gray shreds of paper nest about him like an angry cloud.

A third shot was fired.

The wasps bombarded Berg with white-hot needles, slowing but not stopping the giant as he staggered through the woods.

Fear bubbled in his chest as he ran, but it was sadness that brought fresh tears. Once again, Berg found himself running from those he meant no harm. Panicked and frightened, he couldn't understand the words the men shouted at him, but their intent was enough to break him into a hundred-hundred shards of sorrow.

He heard roaring-river before he saw it. Its growl was large and loud and and powerful. The young giant stepped out of the trees and into the sun, stopping at the edge of a deep ravine. He looked down at roaring-river, its deep waters frosted with whitecaps and swirling currents, telling the story of heavy boulders below the surface.

Berg looked back into the forest and heard the men behind him shouting as they encountered the storm of wasps he'd accidently released. The angry insects were buying him time, but not much. Not enough.

His face and arms burned where the wasps had wounded him, and something warm trickled down the back of his right arm. He rubbed his hand against the spot, and it returned bathed in blood. One of the men's bullets had found its mark.

The gunshot, his escape through the woods, and the venom from a hundred-hundred stings conspired against the young giant. Lights shimmered in his vision, a thousand-thousand specks of blue and green and pink and white. His sturdy knees buckled, and Berg ragdolled down the steep walls of the ravine toward roaring-river.

He found himself at the bottom of the ravine, the icy water assaulting him, and he wondered if he would ever outrun the legend of the giant that had come before him. His worry and fright had turned into disgust for those giants of the past. And as he ran from mob after mob, it was getting more and more difficult to not feel disgusted in himself.

He tried to fight the river, but he was too exhausted. He gave himself to the water and flowed with the current, his cumbersome body limp and powerless against the push and pull of roaring-river. He was as tired as he could ever remember, but he fought to keep his head above the surface, fearing that nothing good would meet him below.

Fatigue sang to him softly, offering rest if he would only close his eyes. Lay back. Sleep.

He let his head dip below the surface. The sound beneath the raging water was subtle, deep, musical. Light filtered through a thousand-thousand bubbles, showing the shimmering silhouettes of boulders. Twin logs stood in the center of the river, dividing the current evenly on either side.

Berg watched the logs as he approached. They seemed to be wading deeper into the river, plodding impossibly toward him.

Fatigue called to him again, her song even sweeter below the surface of roaring-river.

The two logs stopped, rooting themselves in Berg's path. Just before he closed his eyes, the boy-giant saw the logs bend like knees, and a pair of enormous hands plunged below the rushing water to grab him as he gave himself fully to the river.

The young giant slept.

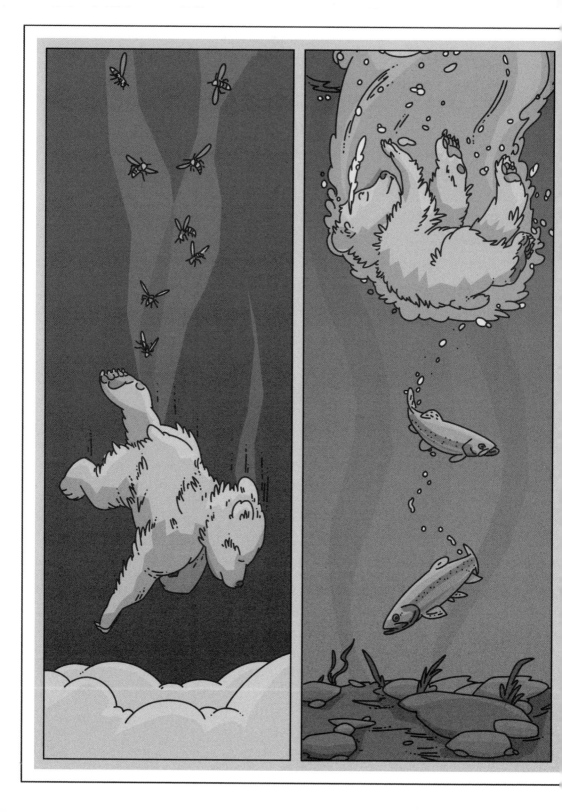

BOOK TWO

WHERE WE LEARN
OF CAVES AND SAND COAXED
FROM THE STARS

AN UNWELCOME CONTRAST

It took strength to open his eyes. His eyelids were swollen, and the stings that covered him burned like a hundred-hundred tiny coals upon his skin. Berg swallowed, trying to send moisture down an impossibly dry throat.

Time had passed since he had been pulled from roaring-river, and the dark of full-night chilled Berg deeply and left him with the shivers. He lay upon his belly, his face pressed against the gravel bank.

A pinch of bright-blue sand rested atop a flat rock a few inches from his nose.

As he looked at the sand, he remembered his dream. The old bear and the young. The river of clouds, the field of grass, and how the old one had pulled a star from the sky and placed it on the young cub's forehead. Berg cleared his throat, then blew the little stack of sand away. The sand twirled into a tornado small enough to spin inside a thimble, then disappeared into the wind.

Night-birds chirped above him, tucked away in nests hidden in the black of trees. Berg rolled to his back, then sat up. He was both burning and freezing, an unwelcome contrast. His satchel lay by his side, and he reached for it but came up short as pain from the bullet burrowed deep into his arm. With gritted teeth and eyes locked closed, he could feel his swollen skin stretch tight across his face.

Berg waited for strength. He hoped for control over the pain. It was new to him—pain like this. The white brightness of it. The red violence of it.

Berg scooted toward his bag. He opened it using his good arm, and he cringed as he noticed his swollen hands. A hundred-hundred angry pink mounds, each crowned with a white dot of pus, threatening to erupt. Carefully, the giant reached inside his bag and checked the contents. One forest-jewel remained. He pulled it out and inspected it. The river stone was pink and triangular, with small crease down the center where time had etched its mark upon the stone. It reminded him of the soft nose of a hare, and he knew it was a rare find indeed.

However, the rabbit-nose-rock resting alone in the center of his large palm seemed lonely to Berg, and at once the pain of his stings seemed to fade compared to the hurt in his heart. The loneliness. The solitude. The heart-pain was worse because he couldn't see it. He couldn't hope to fix it by covering it with mud or wrapping it with bandages. The loneliness was everywhere. It seemed to be in the air around him, in the soil below his wide backside, deep within his blood and bones.

Berg slumped over, his chin resting on his chest, his large paws in the gravel between his legs. He opened his palm and let the rabbit-nose-rock roll to the ground where it joined its new family of riverbank stones.

The giant chided himself for being a fool. For not knowing that the men would come for him. He wondered if they had even noticed his upturned stump. Had they ignored his payment? Were his actions of no value to them? Or had they just chased after him because he was different? Because he was huge, and his size fueled their fear.

Berg looked at the dark mass of trees and rocks of the deep-wild-woods. He listened for the men who had chased him, hurt him, but the deep-wild-woods were silent. The men had gone home.

Berg took in a breath, feeling the cold air deep in his lungs. He looked to the sky to query the stars, but he couldn't see them clearly with a head full of thoughts of wasps, a heart full of sorrow, and a belly full of nothing.

He decided to use his satchel as a makeshift sling for his wounded arm. He lifted it from the river-rock bank and laced it over his wide and dizzy head. His elbow seeped and throbbed as Berg used his good hand to lift his wounded arm through leather loop and place it gingerly on the top of the satchel.

For a moment his vision darkened with pain, and he was certain he would fade away until watchful-moon found her way through the clouds to show him a shimmering something by his side. Lying in rocks in the very spot his satchel had recently been, the silver-brush winked up at Berg. It must have been hiding beneath his satchel, for he knew he would have noticed it earlier.

Berg wondered, in his altered state, if he had stolen the brush after all. But as he watched the moon and clouds roll over the mirrorlike surface of the brush, he knew he had not. Someone else had taken it and placed it by his side.

The silver-brush that once had filled him with desire now left a feeling in his heart as bitter as dandelion greens, and he stood without touching the thing.

He saw the dark shape of a hill ahead, as bare as the crown of an egg. It was the same hill the old bear from his dream had stood upon. Berg knew where to go.

The boy-giant was short of breath when he reached the top of bald-hill. He looked out into the darkness at a quiet valley below. A few lights as small as pinpricks in black velvet blinked at him: orange stars from a hamlet on the other side of a wide valley. Berg scanned the land between him and the distant city, squinting his puffy eyes and listening for sounds of life. Among the rolling shapes of trees and brush, the square body of a barn stood out like a monument.

He waited at the top of the hill. The searing pain in his arm towered above the hundred-hundred stings, and the thought of the men shooting at him returned. Sorrow felt as heavy as stone upon his heart. After running for days, he wanted to make sure the barn was abandoned before he took another chance. The night-birds chirped their songs, letting him know that he was alone, which brought both comfort and sorrow as he stood upon the hill.

A chill visited Berg, as if a ghost had traced its lacy fingers along his spine. A flake of snow pirouetted from the sky and balanced on his bloated nose, where it melted in an instant. Another drifted in front of him, followed by another. The first silent messengers of autumn's passing and winter's promise.

A SECOND BARN

There was no road to travel nor fence to cross as Berg made his way toward the dark barn. A dry field of wheat mixed with brambles and weeds stretched up to touch his knees. Berg reached down and removed a few kernels of wheat. He crunched the rock-hard food, each bite ringing like thunder inside his feverish head. The nuttiness of the grains stirred his appetite and awakened his hope of finding his fill inside the barn.

The rickety shelter slouched to the left. It would take nothing more than a giant's sneeze to topple the tired barn to its final resting spot. Berg leaned his head into the old structure, listening carefully, but his ears returned nothing except the scuttling of night-mice and the never-ending chirp of field-crickets.

He hobbled to the front of the barn. A single pipe with a rusty spigot shaped like a bird stood in the middle of a dry lot. Water dripped from the bird's iron mouth. Berg lifted the handle. Metal creaked as it rose, and then with a gurgle and cough, it spat out rust, then mud, then water as clear as crystal.

Berg found a dented bucket nearby. He filled it time and again, alternately dumping the cold water down his throat, then over his head. He went to his hands and knees, ducking beneath the fountain, where he let the water pour over the stings that covered the back of his neck.

He turned his attention to his gun-shot arm. In the full-dark of night, the blood leaking from the wound was as black and thick as tar. He splashed the hole with water, shivering with every drop.

He stood on wobbly legs. His head hung heavy, and the once-refreshing water froze against his skin. Snowflakes floated around him, their trancelike motion competing for his focus. The young giant reached out with his good hand for balance that wasn't there. Berg squinted his swollen eyes and focused until he saw the open door of the barn behind the falling snow, and with his course set, he plodded forward.

The scent of dust and mice swirled as Berg crossed the threshold of the barn. He half sneezed, a warning that the fever that accompanied him to bald-hill had finally won. He swayed like the twisting snowflakes outside, and then Berg's strength vanished, and he fell to the hard-packed earth with a boom that echoed throughout the valley.

Berg woke.

Infection had nearly glued his eyes shut, but the soft filtered light on his eyelids told Berg that the sun was high in the sky. He managed to open one eye enough to see an impossibility sitting among the flecks of sunlit dust floating in the air.

Parked among geometric stacks of straw was a thousand-thousand pounds of ancient muscle. A giant—much larger, much stronger, much older than Berg—was sitting so close that the boy could smell the rot and ruin even through his stuffed nose. His heart thundered with fear as the figure shifted toward him, and then the ancient giant froze again as still as a statue.

Berg tried to focus on the figure, but the gunk in his eyes made it impossible, like looking through a windowpane coated in honey. All he could see of the figure was his unbelievable size and an outline as soft as smoke. The figure did not move, and Berg hoped beyond hope that his fever was playing tricks. He wished with all his wishes that he was dreaming while awake. He closed his eyes again, tired of the fight, succumbing to sleep's demands.

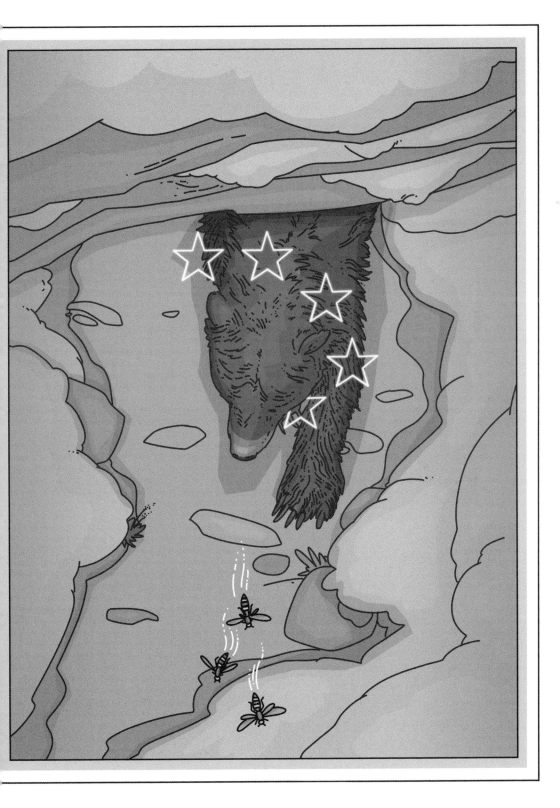

THE BLACKSMITH'S SHACK

Berg woke beneath a blanket of wheat straw. It took effort to open his eyes, but the gunk that had glued them shut earlier was gone. He blinked, then peered at the world through squinted lids. Ocher light trickled in through the cracks in the walls, though it was impossible to tell if it was near-day or near-night. Berg sat up, his head thick and full of slush.

He examined his wounded elbow. The pain was intense, even awesome in its own way. Someone had wrapped his arm in a dingy cloth bandage, making the swollen joint look like the gray globe of a wasp's nest. Visions splashed inside Berg's mind: the hive he'd collided with while escaping the woods, a matching pair of massive hands lifting him from a roaring-river, a silver-brush abandoned on a riverbank.

The pain overwhelmed him, but something teased at his mind beneath the burn. Something he was supposed to do. A task brought to him in a dream of an old bear in the deep-wild-woods.

Berg rose, sloughing off his straw in a golden avalanche. Dust motes danced in the stuffy barn air. He sneezed as he teetered toward the opening.

The battered giant reached out to grab the doorframe to steady himself and saw something dangling from a rope tied to a rusty nail above the doorway. Berg rubbed his eyes with swollen fingers, then blinked until he could focus on the object between him and the outside world. It was a rabbit, roasted recently enough to still be warm. Berg licked his dry and cracked lips. He grabbed the rabbit and pulled it free.

He stepped outside the barn, and his body and bones sensed a soon-to-be storm. It was colder than he'd expected, and he leaned his enormous frame against the barn, feeling weak after only a few steps. He took a bite of the rabbit, and grease ran down his chin and dripped to his chest. With each bite, Berg improved. His strength was a shadow of what it had been before, but even a shadow could bring hope.

He gobbled down the rabbit, bones and all, then licked his oily hands clean. Berg drank his fill of water from the iron spigot, and then he stretched to his full height and his back popped as loud as a tree crashing down in the forest.

His elbow throbbed as blood flushed through his body. Berg looked at the makeshift bandage around his arm. Whoever had wrapped it had probably been the one who cleaned his eyes, buried him beneath straw, and left him the roast rabbit. Berg was in debt. He was grateful for the stranger who had cared for him, and he yearned to repay the favor.

Berg searched the newly fallen snow for tracks. A maze of tiny footprints crisscrossed the yard. Rabbits, cats, foxes—all darting through the snow in pursuit of one another. But no tracks larger than his own thumbprint could be seen. Berg wondered if his rescuer had left before the snow. He wondered if his rescuer would return.

Fog crept across the land. The sun was nowhere to be seen, hidden behind a sky as golden-gray as winter-wool. Berg was still unsure if it was morning or evening. The land around him offered no clue, a monotone landscape impossible to read.

The dark outline of a smaller building no more than a mile away from Berg emerged from the mist. Dark smoke stood like a beacon through the white fog, rising from a chimney in the center of a lonely structure. Perhaps his rescuer was there.

Berg cautiously made his way through the ground-cloud toward the little home.

The acrid smell of burning coal filled the air inside the small shack, and a haze of heavy smoke lingered, nearly as dense as the fog outside. Berg inched carefully indoors, bending over to avoid the wide beams holding the low roof above his head.

He was alone. A fire of orange coals smoldered inside a brick pit in the center of the cluttered shack. Whoever had started the fire must be nearby; no man would dare abandon a thing so hot. So bright.

Rusted swords and shields covered the walls, each hanging from a hook. The blacksmith's tools were scattered around. A hammer with a nose the size of an apple slept on a flat-topped anvil. A collection of rasps filled a wooden box next to a bucket of hand-formed nails. A workbench was littered with iron pliers of every size and shape, looking like a flock of metal bird beaks fixed to the ends of long-handled grips.

As Berg warmed in the smoke-filled shack, he thought about the ancient bear in his dream. He remembered the Dream-Bear standing on his back feet like an old man. An image of the beast tearing into a wasp nest to remove a glowing ember from the center of the hive flickered in his mind.

The dreams were odd to him, for Berg had never been a dreamer. But he didn't question his nightly visions, for they offered him hope, and as he looked at his wounded elbow wrapped in gray swaddling cloth, Berg knew the dream was showing him what to do.

He sifted through the pliers on the workbench until he found a pair with long, curved ends that reminded him of the claws of the ancient bear. He looked at the fire in the smoldering pit. A metal rod nearly three feet long had been stuck in the hot coals. Its tip was the color of the sun, faded to orange, then red, then the flat black of cooled iron. Berg slid to the floor, leaning his back against the workbench, not knowing if he had the strength to stand and perform the task.

He placed the curve-nosed pliers on the ground next to him; then he removed the gray cloth covering his wound. It uncoiled to the floor like a snake shedding its skin. His elbow had swollen to the size of a fat autumn pumpkin, and it was the color of smashed berries.

Berg rolled his arm forward to get a good look at the wound. He bent his elbow, flexing it up and down. The pain was immense as the bullet scratched against bone. He prodded his fingers around the wound, and white light flashed in his eyes as he found the hard bullet beneath his flesh. He picked up the pliers and wiped them on his leg, leaving behind an orange trail of rust upon his thigh.

As he buried the pliers into his arm, he bellowed a scream that rattled the shack. Loose glass panes shook in window frames, and tools and weapons of war fell to the ground all around the giant. He found the angry ball inside his arm, pinched it between the ends of the pliers, and pulled it out and dropped it to the ground, where it rolled into the shadows. Berg dropped the pliers, then slumped back, exhausted, against the workbench.

The blacksmith entered the shop unarmed, but when he saw the blood-covered beast taking up a quarter of the floor of his shop, he quickly filled his hands with a sturdy pickax. He shouted, but Berg struggled to make out what he said as he fought to stay awake.

The blacksmith shouted again. "What are you?"

Berg could not answer.

"Get out. Get out now, or I'll use this pick!"

Berg tried to stand, but it was no use. He fell to his side, his wounded arm overflowing with dark, crimson blood.

The blacksmith approached, quaking with fear and hefting the pickax above his head. "Get out!" he shouted, but Berg didn't hear him as phantom wasps buzzed inside his head and fever swallowed everything but the pain.

A shadow covered the doorway behind the blacksmith, blocking what was left of the cloudy sky. The blacksmith stopped midstride and turned to see what had darkened his workshop. He dropped the pickax as the giant squeezed through the door, cracking it open with his massive shoulders as he passed.

Shock and fear cleared Berg's vision as he watched the giant unroll inside the shack. The giant remained upon his knees and still his shoulders pushed against the ceiling. His face was covered by a beard the color of dingy snow and lined with wrinkles and scars as complex as a sailor's map. He wore thick bearskins, roughly sewn with rawhide, and he smelled of rot and ruin.

The blacksmith toppled over, thumping his head on the edge of the workbench before he slumped like a bag of bones to the hard-packed floor.

The old giant grabbed the blacksmith by his booted foot, then backed out of the shack, dragging the blacksmith behind him. Berg lay with his face against the dirt, unable to move, frozen by fear and fever and fatigue.

The giant returned, grinding through the expanded doorway, then crawling on hands and knees toward Berg. He removed the smoldering iron rod from the blacksmith's fire, grabbing it by the cooled end. Berg thought it looked small in the ancient giant's hands.

The giant approached, the glowing poker in one hand, his other tucked inside the chest of his animal-fur coat. When he reached Berg, the giant removed his hand from his bearskin covering, and a few flecks of star-blue-sand leaked from the corners of his fist. He opened his hand, then blew.

A small pile of star-blue-sand danced and twirled into a ballerina's pirouette, leaving behind tiny specks of starlight as it traveled through the air toward the young giant.

Berg closed his eyes as the star-blue-sand approached, and he never saw the inside of the blacksmith's shack again.

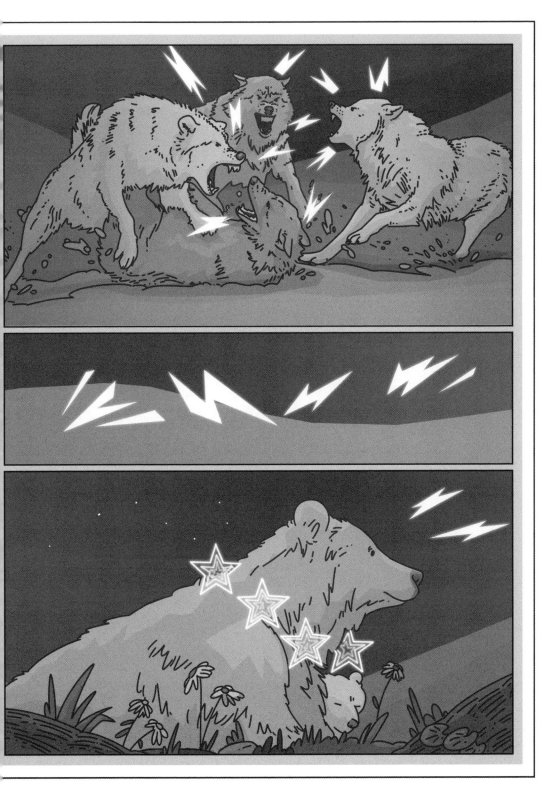

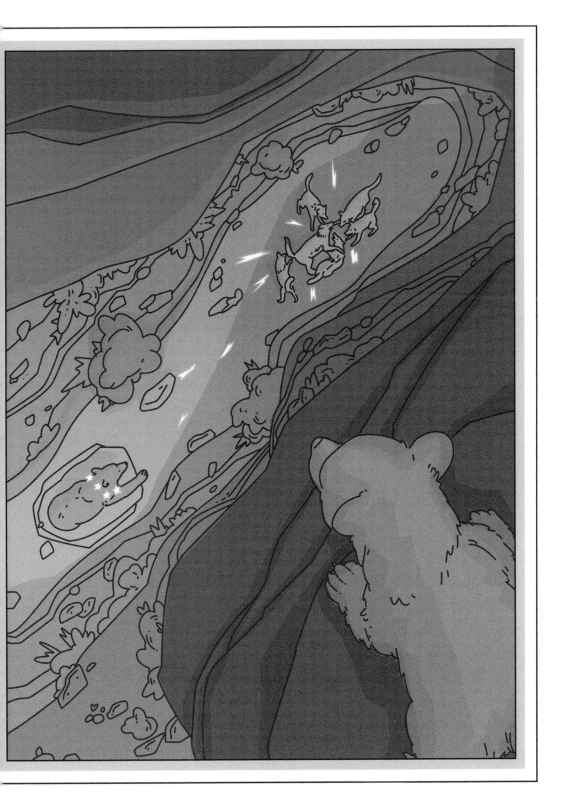

A CAVE FILLED WITH STARS

Berg stirred in a world of black, waking as slow as a hibernating bear. His young heart was filled with fear. The last thing he remembered was the giant with the smoking, hot iron and fleeting images of being carried through the woods upon the giant's back. Berg was alone and lost and frightened by the dark that ate him up.

The smell of damp shadows was familiar to Berg. He'd slept in caves before, but this cave was unknown to him. He listened in the dark, asking his ears to help him find his way. Water dripped in perfect rhythm from the top of the cave into an unseen pool; the echo from the well-timed drops told Berg the cave was large. He was alone in the cave. He heard no bats above him scratching and screeching. Berg knew, even in the dark, that it was full-night, and the bats were out chasing night-bugs and stealing bites of fruit.

He pressed his big hands against the floor to push himself up, then checked his elbow to inspect the wound. The pain was nearly gone, and a soft scab the size of a walnut was beginning to form. He hinged his elbow open and closed, pleased to find it working well and free of aches and pains. Berg used both hands to check his face and neck and arms. The wasp stings that had once covered him had all but gone, leaving behind hard mounds upon his skin. The poison that accompanied them had nearly disappeared.

He went to his knees and used his hands to feel around in the dark, searching the soft floor of the cave for his satchel. He had lost it sometime during his pain-filled stupor but hoped his bag would still be nearby. He hadn't realized until it was gone how much he loved the satchel. It was all he had from his youth; he'd outgrown or torn most of his clothing, he'd traded everything else away for food and drink, and now he feared his leather satchel was gone as well. Lost and gone forever.

Berg crawled toward the sound of dripping water, unable to stay put in the dark any longer. He found the edge of the cave with his right shoulder first when he scraped it against a damp wall. He used the wall to guide him as he inched forward in the black.

The floor beneath him lost its padding as he worked his way from the bat cavern and into a long corridor where his shoulders touched the walls on both sides. The hallway continued to narrow as he followed the path, forcing Berg to stand and walk sidestep. In a few more steps, his chest and back touched the cave walls. He pushed ahead, scraping his skin, the cave's toll for allowing him to pass.

The young giant was nearly ready to turn back and search for another way out when he saw an odd, blue glow ahead.

He pushed through the cramped pass and into a roomy corridor, then stepped cautiously toward the faint, flickering light. Sapphire flecks glimmered within the cavern walls. Berg brushed his hands against the wall, and particles clung to his skin, glowing like stars in a night sky. It was the sand, the star-blue-sand he'd seen in his dreams. He looked deeper into the cave, and the blue glow intensified, the star-blue-sand coating the walls.

Berg sniffed, smelling the perfume of a cook fire and roasted meat in the air. The demand to fill his belly pushed him forward into the cave filled with stars, but as he approached, he realized he was no longer alone.

He heard the breathing of the beast. The rotten smell of him stole away the scent of cook fire and meat. Berg was tired of being alone, but the thought of being trapped in the cave with the ancient giant filled him with fear beyond anything he'd ever imagined.

He knew who the beast was—Ünhold the Giant. The very giant whose tales of destruction had haunted Berg for as long as he could remember. It was the legend of Ünhold the Giant that had forced Berg to live a life of loneliness and despair.

Berg found a corner and did his best to hide himself while Ünhold shuffled around and grunted like a bear, just out of sight. The fire hissed as it was extinguished, and Berg held his breath as he saw the outline of the beast cross the threshold between his hiding spot and the room filled with stars. Ünhold raised his hands above his head and tied a roasted rabbit to a rusted hook hammered into the ceiling of the cave.

The blue dust that covered the walls gave off little light, but even in the near-dark Berg could see the scowl on the beast's face. His beard and hands were covered in the dust, glowing faintly as he finished tying the knot around the metal hook. The giant ducked beneath the rabbit he'd secured, and then Berg held his breath and imagined he was a rock as Ünhold passed by him and walked toward the room where Berg had slept with the bats.

He heard the ancient giant squeeze through the narrow passageway and wondered how someone nearly twice his size could fit through a spot that had nearly trapped him. Berg didn't wait for Ünhold's return. He rose to his feet, then yanked the freshly cooked rabbit from the hook as he passed from his hiding spot into the massive room.

Berg froze, awestruck at the beauty around him. A large hole opened in the top of the cave, and the splinter-moon and a billion stars stared down at him. Berg followed the moon's glow to the center of the room, where a gigantic blue-black stone was embedded deep in the floor and surrounded by a desert of star-blue-sand.

He walked to the stone and placed a rough hand upon its smooth surface. He'd never seen one before, but the moment he touched the blue-black monolith he knew he was in the company of a fallen star. He looked at the sky and imagined the star ripping through the mountain's thick crust to find the cave.

Berg knelt and buried his hands in the star-blue-sand. All his sadness from being alone and his fright at the monster in the cave faded away as he raked his fingers through the sand. Visions filled his bright mind—a small bear waking next to his mother, a pack of sleeping wolves, a white bear pulling blue stardust from inside a leather satchel. He saw the splinter-moon high in the sky, and he felt as if the moon were reaching out to comfort him. For a moment, with his hands buried in stardust, Berg was happy. Berg was content.

He was nearly lost in a dreamlike trance when he heard the scraping of Ünhold returning through the narrow throat of the cave. Berg yanked his hands from the sand, and cold fear returned in a flood.

Berg retrieved the cooked rabbit he'd dropped by his side, took a small handful of the star-blue-sand, and climbed to the top of the fallen star. From his elevated station, he could easily reach the edge of the hole the star had carved in the earth. He tested his strength for the first time since he'd been shot in the woods. It hadn't fully returned, but enough remained for him to pull himself up and out of the hole. Berg heard the beast enter the blue room just as he breached the outside world.

Berg rose from the cave to find himself at the top of a formidable mountain. The splinter-moon was stingy with her light, only providing Berg with hints and whispers of the descent before him. In one hand, he clutched the star-blue-sand, seeking its strength, soaking in its hope.

The night was clear and cool, and as Berg worked his way down the mountain, he entered a clearing in the forest. Far away on the floor of a vast valley lay the unmistakable glow of streetlights burning in a sleeping town. He looked back up toward Ünhold and his cave of stars.

Berg weighed the fears in his heart: going back would bring him face-to-face with the beast who smelled of rot and ruin, but moving on would lead him to another town of people who could mock him. Chase him. Poke him with pitchforks, or much worse.

But there was always the chance that the people in the new town had never heard of the legend of Ünhold the Giant. And if that were the case, they might be willing to give Berg a chance to show them who he really was. And while a chance couldn't fill a giant's belly, for Berg a chance offered something more.

Hope.

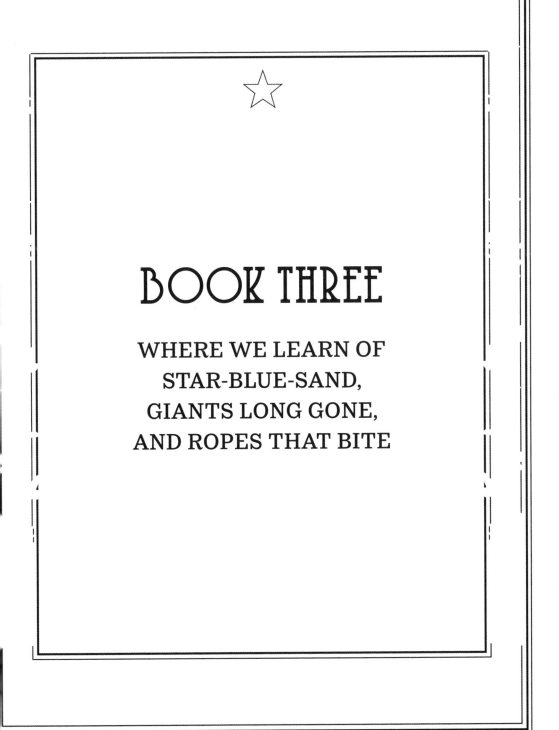

BOOK THREE

WHERE WE LEARN OF
STAR-BLUE-SAND,
GIANTS LONG GONE,
AND ROPES THAT BITE

A DASH OF SAND

He traveled at night as the sky turned gray, hurrying toward the town in hopes of finding food before the sun lent light to the world. He arrived as the splinter-moon slipped shyly behind a cloud. Berg hid in a field of tall grass away from the eyes of flickering flames in iron baskets that hung from posts surrounding the city wall.

The wall itself was made of iron, a fortress of wide panels of black and rusted metal bound together with hammered rivets the size of mushroom caps. The metal wall was as tall as a dogwood forest, and it offered neither foothold nor handle, an unclimbable barrier between Berg and the city within. Angry iron spikes grew from the city wall like a crown of thorns. A metal bridge spanned a river gorge and led to a gate of iron and wood.

Above the gate, the snarling face of a wolf gargoyle stood guard. A fire burned inside the wolf, orange light flickering from within its angry eyes and tooth-lined mouth. Two night guards, dressed in chain mail and fine tapestry tunics, stood atop the wall above the fire-grinning-wolf, warming their hands and yawning above its flames as snow began to fall.

Berg watched the lazy guards, and before long, their chatting ceased. The guards stoked the snarling gargoyle with a load of coal, then slept beneath their tunics to keep their heads dry from the snow.

Berg waited until his hunger outweighed the risk of being caught. He crossed the field of grass, then moved quiet as a cloud-shadow across the bridge. The fire-grinning-wolf glared down at Berg, warning him to stay away, but the boy-giant paid the iron sculpture no mind. Snowflakes hissed as they landed on the skull of the wolf, sending puffs of steam in the air as Berg crept beneath the wolf to stand in front of the city gate.

Thick iron bars were bolted through the rough-hewn planks of a heavy oak door. Berg squatted, positioning his powerful legs wide apart. His fingertips found a grip beneath one of the iron bars. He placed his chest and face against oak, then heaved upward with one hand. The gate rose as Berg stood. He braced a knee beneath the gate, then slid his hand under the lip of the stalwart wall and raised it up until it locked into place above his head.

Berg entered the walled city, standing on a cobblestone street that stretched out before him. The splinter-moon found a crack in the clouds and shined off the street's wet surface like a thousand-thousand scales on the back of a long black snake.

The town was silent. Not a soul walked the streets, so Berg crept forward, anxious at the thought of being spotted. High-pitched roofs converged in narrow peaks designed to slough off the snow that would soon cover the city. The windows were boarded up with thick metal shutters, latched together from the inside, something the giant had never seen before. Berg's stomach ached, and his face drooped with disappointment at the sight of the sealed-up homes.

While imagining treasures of food hidden inside the private homes, Berg accidentally kicked a tin cup in the gutter, knocking it down the street with a clang that rang like a cymbal. Berg froze, but when the rattle hadn't woken the townsfolk, he retrieved the cup and emptied what remained of the star-blue-sand he held into it.

He worked his way through town until he stopped at an eerie mansion with dragon gargoyles that sneered at Berg from the roof. The windows of the massive home were locked with ornately sculpted iron shutters. But even iron couldn't hold back the scent of fresh-baked bread inside the home.

Berg's mouth watered as he placed the tin cup on the windowsill, his stomach driving his actions. Hunger shoved fear out of Berg's mind, and he jammed his fingernails beneath the metal shutters, ignoring the idea of being discovered. He pried against the stubborn window until his nails cracked. His hunger turned sour, demanding he try again. Berg bit back a growl and pulled harder against the window until it flung open with a crack, surprising the young giant and knocking over the tin cup of star-blue-sand.

Sorrow flew in on a little wind toward Berg, the breath blowing away the star-blue-sand faster than he could scoop it back into the cup with his huge, clumsy fingers. He had hoped to keep the sand and perhaps hold it again when he felt lonely, hidden away in the deep-wild-woods. But much to his surprise, the precious particles began to dance.

At first, only a few grains of the star-blue-sand played along, chasing each other in a circle the size of a coin. But soon the others joined in, spinning in the air an inch above the windowsill.

Berg watched with his mouth agape and his eyes wide as the sand formed a twirling tornado no bigger than a thimble. The twirling sand was the most beautiful thing he'd ever seen. He reached out to catch it, but the blue tornado escaped and gracefully spun through the open window and continued to pirouette inside the home.

Berg was hypnotized by the whirligig motion of the star-blue-sand, completely lost to its mysteries as it twirled above the loaves of bread. The dancing sand slipped down a dark hallway, and the young giant felt more alone than he had in a great-long time. He missed the spinning sand and its twirling dance. He wanted it back to hold in his hands.

Berg waited for the tiny tornado to return, but a man entered the room instead. At the sight of him, Berg ducked beneath the window to stay out of view. He closed his eyes and covered his chest to hide the drumming of his heart as he listened to the man fumbling around inside the home.

The hush of well-oiled hinges told Berg the window above him was opening further, and the man's voice mumbled a few feet from the young giant's head.

Curiosity pried open Berg's eyes, and, without moving from his spot, he tilted his head up and saw the man leaning out of the window.

His mustache was black and shiny like a licorice stick, but perfectly curled at the ends as if the man slept rigidly upon his back. His jaw was slack and his eyes were closed in a relaxed manner that told Berg the man was still asleep. In his arms, he held one of the large loaves of bread and as many apples as he could carry. The sleepwalker's mustache twitched just before he yawned, then he dropped the food directly upon Berg's startled head.

The young giant sat beneath the window and watched in utter amazement as the sleepwalker pulled the window closed and disappeared into his home.

Berg waited until the city was silent once again before crouching to gather the apples and the loaf of bread. Happiness filled the giant as he crunched into an apple, the juice spilling from his mouth and dripping from his chin. Sitting in the street, his back against the mansion, he marveled at the trade he'd just made.

He was lost in thought, occasionally lifting the bread up to his nose for a whiff, when something tiny and brave spoke.

"Who are you?"

Berg bucked, startled by the little girl, but she didn't flinch as she stood in the street next to him. She balanced a ladder over her shoulder; its back rungs fixed to a child's wagon twenty feet behind her. With a curious smile lifting the corners of her mouth, the young girl stared up at Berg, and his heart stopped. He'd dreamed of this moment for as long as he could remember. But now that it was here, now that one of the small ones was standing beside him, unafraid and interested, Berg was too alarmed to speak.

THE GIRL IN THE STREET

Berg did not dare look directly at the girl standing below him. Instead, he found himself studying the sealed windows of the homes across the street. He held his breath and tried to think like a boulder, hoping the girl would leave quietly when she realized she was looking at a giant and not scream to call the townsfolk. Fear and hope wrestled inside him, for although he was terrified, the largest part of him wished with all his might that she would stay.

"Hello?" Her voice was soft and pure, without a trace of the worry or hatred he'd heard in other voices in the past. "Can you hear me?"

Sunshine seemed to burst through Berg's massive heart, and he nodded without looking at the girl, his eyes tightly closed. He heard her take a few steps closer, the wheels of her wagon squeaking far behind her. Thoughts zipped around inside Berg's mind. He wondered about the ladder she carried. He wondered why she was awake so late at night. He wondered why she hadn't run away to fetch the others.

"Did he give you that? The mayor. Did he give you the bread and apples?" Berg nodded again.

"Who are you?"

A single eyelid lifted, and Berg braved a peek at the girl. Her hair was so orange it still held its color in the light of the splinter-moon. Berg closed his eyes again.

"It's okay. You can look at me."

Berg turned his head a little and looked down at the girl in the street.

She smiled wide, and he noticed a dusting of freckles across her face. She waved, then placed her end of the ladder in the street. "My name is Anya. What do they call you?"

Berg wondered who *they* were. Other people called him giant, troll, beast. They called him Ünhold. But there was no way he was going to tell that to the girl. He hated those names because they were not who he was. He wanted to tell her what he called himself, but she spoke again, asking him a question that caused him to open his eyes wide in amazement.

"Do all the giants have magic sand?"

Questions flew so fast through Berg's head that he couldn't catch a single one and bring it to his mouth, but his silence wasn't a problem for the girl.

Anya carried on their one-sided conversation. "Do you have any more?"

Berg shook his head.

"That's too bad. I wish I had a whole bucket full of it all for myself. But that's silly, isn't it?" She fished a small rope necklace out from beneath her coat's collar. A vial, no larger than the girl's smallest finger, was tied to the end, and in the bottom lay a small girl's pinch of star-blue-sand. She lifted it to show Berg. "This is all I've got. I've been waiting for the old giant to return, but he hasn't been back for five days."

Berg glanced at the necklace and the star-blue-sand, then flashed a glance at the ladder in the street.

"I don't steal the sand," Anya said as she followed his glance. "I wait until the old giant is gone, and then I climb up to the windows and dust up what he left behind. If you had more, I could show you a trick."

Berg tilted his head and furrowed his brow. The girl had him in a trance. He took every word she said as if it were a fine gift.

He'd seen the sand twirl into the fancy home behind him, but he hadn't done anything special; the sand had done it on its own. He wanted to know what trick the girl could do with the sand, and he wished he'd not been so clumsy. He wished more than anything he'd ever hoped for that he had more of the sand to give to the girl so she could show him her trick and, perhaps, spend just a little more time with her.

"You know, there are better things than bread and apples," Anya said with a smile.

Berg tilted his head the other way, and his eyebrows shot up in response. The girl laughed. The playful sound tickled Berg's ears, and he rubbed one of them with his wide palm.

"You sure say a lot without opening your mouth. Follow me. I'll show you."

The girl picked up her ladder again, balancing one end expertly on her shoulder, the other end still tied to the wagon. Berg stayed far behind as she led him through the city. He didn't want his shadow to swallow up the moon and cover the girl's bright orange hair with his darkness.

Anya led Berg past the center of town and onto a small street lined with shops. She walked with a confidence Berg envied as he followed her with his usual stooped creep. The uneasiness that had haunted the giant earlier returned as he noticed how empty the streets were. He wanted to ask Anya about the strange town, but he couldn't fish the right words out of his excited mind.

Hand-carved signs hung from twisted iron poles, identifying what the stores offered. Berg had seen shops before, but this new city was far grander than the others. A pink hog adorned one sign, a pair of shoes another, a round pie complete with rising steam was painted on yet another, and many more were covered with items and objects Berg didn't recognize.

The young girl stopped in front of a shop with a sign showing a red ball fixed to the end of a long white stick, and Berg wondered what things were kept inside. Anya used her ladder to climb to a shuttered window, then motioned for him to join her. He crept to her side, feeling the cool cobblestone street beneath his feet. Moonlight shined off her freckled face, and Berg leaned in to hear her whisper.

"This is Bartle Brickle's Sweetshop. He's the finest candymaker in all of Eisenstadt. I think I have just enough sand left to do one last trick. Should we try?"

The words played like songbirds in Berg's ears, and he nodded. He didn't understand exactly what she said, but he could tell by the cheerful way she'd raised her eyebrows that whatever was inside the shop would be a treasure indeed.

Anya pulled out her necklace again, then removed the tiny cork from the top of the vial and poured the star-blue-sand out on the windowsill. She inched toward the little pile, puckered her lips, and blew. Her breath caught the sand, and it began to dance and twirl. This time the window remained sealed, but that didn't hinder the magical sand. It spun through the thick metal shutters like a spirit.

The sand was astonishing, but Berg couldn't stop watching Anya. Her face seemed to glow as she watched the sand spin, and Berg felt something warm growing inside him, starting deep inside his chest and slowly radiating through his entire body. He had never been as happy as he was at that very moment. He watched as Anya put her feet on the outside rails of the ladder; then she slid down where she landed silently on the cobblestone street below.

Someone inside the candymaker's shop fumbled with heavy metal locks behind the window.

"Here he comes," Anya said as she motioned for Berg to hide. He took a step and slid between the candy shop and the building next door, his head and shoulders rising above their high-pitched roofs.

A round man with a bushy beard and a head as bald as an egg appeared as the shutters swung open. His eyes were closed. In his hand, he held a red-and-white-striped sack. It hung from his hand for a second, and then he loosened his grip and the bag dropped. Anya held out her hands and caught the bag as if she and the candymaker had practiced a hundred-hundred times before.

She did a little dance in the street, celebrating the treasure she held in her hands as the sleeping candymaker closed his window and disappeared into the dark home.

Anya waved at the vanished candymaker, then placed the red-and-white bag in her wagon and wheeled it over to Berg.

"Come on. Grab my ladder, will ya?" She hurried down the street, her wagon squeaking like a stuttering mouse.

Berg, afraid the noisy wagon would bring the candymaker to his window again, watched the girl walk away. She stopped and motioned for him to follow, and although he was certain they would be discovered, he picked up the ladder and joined her.

She took him to the center of town, where she sat next to a large fountain. She patted the ground next to her, and Berg thought she might want him to sit. He was amazed by the brave way she walked through town with him, as if nobody would think it was wrong for the two of them to be together, as if he were no different from anyone else. As if he belonged.

"Wait until you try these. They are the best." She dug to the bottom of the bag and pulled out a small handful of what Berg thought looked like yellow stones. She held out her hand. "Go on. These are for you."

Berg reached out and placed his hand beneath hers. She touched him as she let the yellow stones roll into his palm, and the sunshiny feeling returned, rolling through him like a tide.

"Go on, silly. Eat them. They're called lemon drops. They're my favorite."

Berg's eyes were full, and a tear the size of a fat blackberry ran down his cheek and dropped in his lap. She had given him something without him paying first. She had talked to him and showed him her sand trick, which was better than his because the candymaker's window had remained closed. She had led him through the city without letting the others know he was there, but all of this seemed to shrink because she had touched him. He swallowed as another tear fell to his lap.

"What's wrong? It's just candy." Anya held up a small red ball balanced on the end of a white stick, just like the sign above the candymaker's shop. "This is a lollipop. My next favorite." She plopped the treat in her mouth to show Berg it was safe.

Berg put the lemon drops in his mouth, and his eyes opened wide and, without knowing he'd done it, he smiled.

"Told you there were things better than bread."

Berg nodded again.

She held up the bag. "All this for a pinch of dream-sand. Pretty good trade if you ask me. The candymaker gets a night filled with perfect dreams, and I get a sack full of goodies."

The words *dream-sand* played through Berg's mind. Memories he couldn't quite catch of his mother, and dreams, and her satchel full of star-blue-sand. Berg let out a breath, not realizing he'd been holding it in.

"I'd better go home," Anya said. "I need to be in bed before my uncle wakes up, or I'll be in a lot of trouble. Want to give me a lift?"

Berg didn't know what she was talking about, but he nodded anyway.

"I've always wanted to ride a giant."

Berg understood, and he smiled again. She stood and dusted off her backside. He offered up his hand, and she climbed aboard. The young giant lifted her to his shoulder, where she sat and grabbed on to a tuft of his wild hair.

A new feeling rose inside of him, one he couldn't remember feeling before, yet he knew its name. Somehow four apples, a loaf of bread, and three small yellow candies had been able to do what no meal had ever done. Berg was full.

Anya giggled as they rose above the city, her laugh tickling Berg's ear.

"I can't believe this. You get to see this all the time. You are so lucky," she said, and for the first time in his life, Berg was grateful to be tall.

"I live there—in the house where you got the apples."

Berg returned to the house with the dragon gargoyles. She directed him around back where a tall spire rose. While standing in the middle of Berg's hand, Anya reached out and opened the shuttered window. She climbed inside her room, then turned around and looked at him eye to eye.

"I leave this one unlocked," she said with a smile. She held out the red-and-white-striped sack of candy. "Go on. I want you to have the rest."

Berg took the bag and cupped it against his chest with his giant hand. He nodded his thanks. He was turning to leave when she spoke again.

"Hey, wait. What's your name?"

Berg wasn't sure he wanted to speak. In only a few unspoiled minutes, this night had become the most amazing treasure he owned. He feared if he spoke he would ruin everything. He was afraid if she heard his huge voice that she'd shut her window and lock it tight, or worse, that Anya might disappear, and he'd learn that the entire night had been nothing more than a dream. A perfect, lovely dream he'd earned by carrying the star-blue-sand.

"I don't want to call you 'giant' anymore. I want to know your name."

The young giant swallowed, then whispered in his most hushed tone, "I am Berg."

The girl smiled at the sound of his name.

"Nice to meet you, Berg. You come back again. Okay?" she said with a smile as warm as summer-sun.

Berg nodded, stunned again by the girl and the way she didn't seem to mind that he was a giant. With his belly feeling full and his heart hammering against his chest, Berg told her a secret.

"I know where to get more star-blue-sand."

"Oooh. Really? Well then, we can have fun, you and me. Little Anya and Berg the Giant."

Berg nodded as his eyes began to water again. He was too filled with joy to stop the tears from rolling down his cheeks as he ran from the walled city before the sun came up, promising to return with a red-and-white-striped bag full of star-blue-sand.

THE GIANT'S STORE

The mountain that held Ünhold's cave tested Berg's strength, but his desire to return to Anya with more star-blue-sand fueled him. Snow fell as he climbed throughout the daylight hours, and the wind howled and tossed Berg's hair, making his trek up the mountain even more dangerous than his descent the night before. His back and legs ached from the climb. It was more than he was accustomed to, and he marveled at the strength it would have required for Ünhold to carry him up the rocky path.

Berg hadn't slept in quite some time, and with the excitement and confusion of the last day, his mind was filled with thoughts. He wondered why the old giant had helped him. He knew by the rabbit he'd taken from the cave the night before that Ünhold had been the one to leave the rabbit for him in the barn. He was certain Ünhold had also been the one who had wrapped his wound, which meant that the other giant had also carried him to his cave while Berg slept his fever away.

The girl, Anya, also seemed to know about the old giant. She didn't say as much, but it didn't seem like she was afraid of Ünhold. And it was obvious, and joyfully so, that Anya wasn't afraid of Berg either.

But such thoughts made no sense to the young giant. Berg had lived his life running away from the stories of the old one who smelled of rot and ruin. He knew the giant was bad, angry, and dangerous beyond compare.

With fear shadowing his every decision, Berg paused at the entrance of the cave and listened. He couldn't wait to bring back the dream-sand to Anya and the people of the town, but he was terrified of the old giant inside the cave. Snores growled, and Berg began to shake. He had hoped Ünhold would be out hunting around the mountainside, but sleeping was the next best thing. He wiped his brow, clearing melted snow and sweat from his eyes.

From his vantage point outside the top of the cave, the sand looked as ordinary as valley dirt. The fallen star appeared to be nothing more than an exposed column of common coal. Berg lowered himself into the cave, reaching down with icy toes to stand on the fallen star. The surface was wet and cold, and he slipped, dropping to the floor with a thud.

The old giant grunted, and Berg's heart jumped into his throat. Lying in the sand with the bag of treats in his hand, the young giant dared not move. He waited, barely breathing, until the ancient one began to snore again.

Taking a moment to really look at the beast for the first time, Berg's fear compounded as he studied his strength and size. Ünhold's eyebrows met in the center of his wrinkled face, and he was dressed in furs he'd obviously sewn himself. Berg wore nothing more than an old wrap of cloth that he had found tied to a tree near a city far away, but he wouldn't have traded the warmth it offered for the filth and fleas accompanying the old giant's clothes. His age was evident upon his face, but an exposed arm displayed the muscles of a much younger giant as veins meandered over his forearms and paw-like hands.

Swallowing his fear, Berg crawled toward Ünhold and emptied the bag of candies to trade, lining up the goodies in a neat row. Ünhold belched, filling the cave with rancid gas that smelled of onions and sour milk.

Berg backed away from the odorous beast, then filled the paper sack with star-blue-sand. He stood, ready to climb from the cave of stars, when he saw a second tunnel he hadn't noticed before leading away from the center of the cave. Fear still dwelt in the cave with Berg, but he was encouraged by the deep sleep that covered Ünhold. He decided to chance his luck, and he crept toward the unexplored tunnel, ducking low to let himself in.

The light inside the second room was dim, but enough leaked in to reveal the treasures within. Berg dared not enter fully, for fear of tipping over the piles and piles of riches before him. Stacks of copper bowls gleamed on a table too small for giants. A hill of wire birdcages was placed before a leaning tower of leather-bound books. Flour sacks were scattered about, filled with anything but flour. Apples, potatoes, onions, and beets poured from some, gold and silver coins overflowed from others. Berg's head pressed against the ceiling of Ünhold's treasure room as he studied the contents, trying to guess how much star-blue-sand the giant must have traded to assemble such a magnificent collection.

He looked at the bag of sand in his hand. It was beautiful and magic, but he knew all the sand in the cave was nothing compared to the stacks and piles of riches before him. He knew as he gawked at Ünhold's riches that the stories he'd heard were true. The giant was a thief.

Berg's bag of star-blue-sand felt heavy as he looked at Ünhold's store. He had taken too much. He wanted to bring the sand to Anya and her townsfolk, but he didn't want to do it like this. He didn't want to be a thief, like Ünhold. He emptied half the bag of star-blue-sand, weighing it in his hands to judge when the amount weighed as much as the candy he had left for Ünhold; then he took his leave.

Halfway down the mountain, Berg passed a comfortable-looking spot beneath the outstretched arms of a massive pine. The relief from collecting the star-blue-sand without being caught by Ünhold left him feeling tired beyond measure. Looking back at the top of the mountain that held the sleeping giant, Berg listened. Nothing returned but the creaking of trees being rocked by the mountain wind. He held the small bag of sand to his chest, then curled beneath the tree and slept.

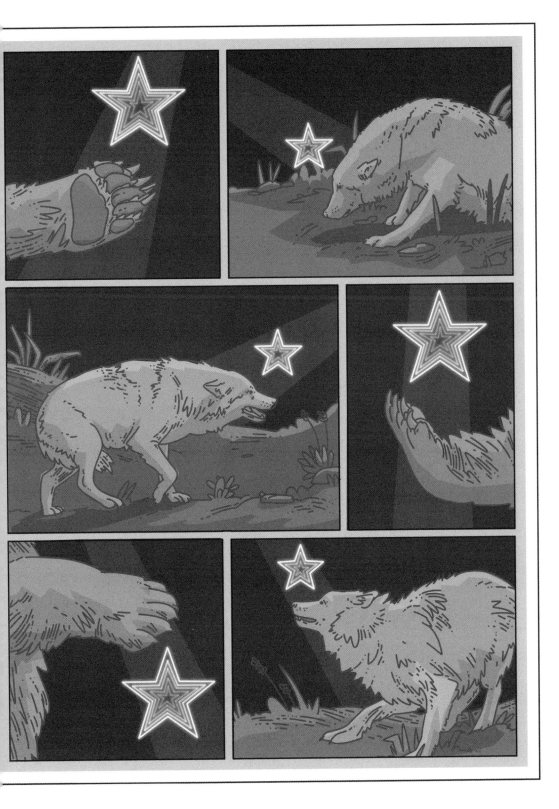

AN UNWELCOME OFFERING

The young giant had never entered a city during the day, but this was not just any day.

Not wanting to arrive as unclean or as unruly as Ünhold, Berg decided he would wash himself before entering the iron-city. After wading into the river that bordered the city, he submerged himself below the rusted bridge, hiding in the shadows as a horse-drawn cart passed overhead. He plucked handfuls of coarse reeds and used them to scrub the black from his hands, his knees, his elbows. He tried his best to calm his wild hair, pulling his fingers through knots and snarls, until the top of his head ached where the roots had nearly been tugged from his scalp.

Berg removed his wrappings, then rubbed them through the reeds and water until the dingy brown cloth looked nearly as white as it had the day he had found it. He wrapped the cloth around him and secured it with a knot as wide as a melon.

He climbed from the moat as clean as he'd ever been, grabbed the red-and-white-striped bag he'd left on the bank, and crossed the bridge toward the iron wall. The fire-grinning-wolf gargoyle atop the open gates scowled down at him. It was sooty and black and reeked of brimstone, a more imposing guardian in the daylight than it had been the night before.

Berg held the bag of sand in his hand, the dream of the star-topped-wolves in his mind and the memory of Anya in his heart. He had intended to wait until nighttime, but as he plodded through the woods and neared the iron-city, Berg convinced himself that if a pinch of sand could win over Anya, then ten times as much would surely convince the townsfolk that he was kind. That he was good.

From outside the wall, Berg could see the cobblestone street had been swept clean of snow. Carts of food were manned by merchants in neat rows on either side of the stone road. Townsfolk bustled about, haggling for goods and chatting like a flock of greedy geese.

Berg ducked below the chin of the iron wolf gargoyle to avoid hitting his head, and as he entered, the city stopped.

A hundred-hundred cold eyes, wide and round and full of shock, stared at Berg as he paused at the entrance of the city, his clothes and hair dripping with water. The movements he saw were subtle and cautious. Mothers pushed children behind full skirts, men tightened their hands around broomsticks or wood-handled knives, children covered their eyes with their hands or whispered to one another like conspirators.

Berg watched and waited, turning his square head slightly to look into the faces of the townsfolk. They diverted their eyes as his gaze landed upon them, cowering at the sight of the massive giant.

He saw her then—Anya, her hair glowing bright in the high sun. She walked into the street and brushed her hands toward him in a shooing motion. Berg couldn't quite make out if it was a wave or a warning, so he tried to smile, and the crowd cringed. All except the red-haired girl, who swooshed her hands at him again and mouthed something silently into the air.

Berg had not thought beyond entering the town, but as he looked at the market, he remembered his dream of the small bear and the den of wolves. He had come to offer the sand in trade for their trust. The promise of wonderful dreams for a welcome place to stay, a home to call his own. As he stood in the town, dripping like a rain cloud, Berg grew confident, for although the people weren't inviting him in, they were not shouting at him or chasing him away either.

Berg attempted to smile, but this time he leaned forward, crouching down to meet them, his arms out wide to show he was kind. He bared his teeth to show them they were not as yellow and chipped as Ünhold's.

The townsfolk recoiled and collected in small huddles. Berg saw the man with the waxed mustache tuck Anya under his arm and hurry her away from the market. Her eyes found his for a second, and he wanted to call out her name, to ask her to explain to the people that he was kind.

He opened his mouth the tiniest crack to speak when a man dressed in tan, loose-fitting clothing covered in white powder pulled a large loaf of bread from the top of his wooden cart.

The keeper-wolves dream came to Berg's mind again, and he mimicked the vision by opening his bag and pouring a tiny pile of the star-blue-sand to the ground before the baker. To his amazement, the sand remained in place. Not a single speck twirled or spun in the air.

The dusty man walked slowly toward Berg, the bread held out in front of him in both hands. The baker tossed the golden loaf to the cobblestone street, then scampered back to join the crowd, never taking his eyes off Berg and ignoring the sand altogether.

"You take! You go!" the baker shouted as he motioned with both hands, copying the gesture Anya had performed when he had first entered the town. The baker's words were hurtful. They were rough and simple, and he spoke as if Berg was nothing but a wild dog.

Berg inched forward, his rough feet scraping on the cobblestones. He knelt and picked up the loaf between his thumb and forefinger. The bread was fragrant and warm, and to show his gratitude, he tossed it into his mouth. Three chews and one gulp later, he stood and nodded gratefully to the crowd, who continued to watch the giant in fear.

Berg took a step toward them, and they moved back as one. He looked down at a man with a honey cart, his bees floating happily through the air. Berg poured a half-teaspoon of the sand on the edge of the beekeeper's cart. He remembered Anya blowing on the sand the night before, and he gave the little pile a tender puff, but once again the star-blue-sand refused to do its dance.

The anxious beekeeper opened the hive and pulled out a wedge of honeycomb. He dusted off the bees, then passed the sticky treat to Berg.

The giant took it and chomped it down, savoring the sugary goodness as it filled his mouth and ran down his throat. He tilted his head back and tried to laugh. It was the first time he remembered doing it in his entire life, but he knew how wonderful it felt when he heard Anya laugh the night before.

But the people of the iron-city did not seem as delighted with his laugh. They flinched, and a few of them shrieked, but Berg could feel a seed of hope growing inside him. The people were offering him food in trade for his star-blue-sand, even though the sand refused to delight them with its spinning trick.

Berg looked around the city, studying the remaining carts. They were piled high with fruits and baked goods and ceramic urns filled with sweet-smelling drinks. He felt the weight of the sand in his bag, knowing he had plenty to treat everyone in town to a pinch of their own.

He was trying to decide which cart to visit next when the first rope wrapped around his neck. His paper sack of star-blue-sand spilled as the second rope grabbed his wrist. Pain turned the young giant around as the ropes bit into his skin. He grabbed at the one around his neck, then spun to look at the people, wrapping himself up in the ropes at his own peril.

Men and boys swung more ropes in aggressive arcs, a metal claw fixed to the end of each. The crowd cheered as a third biting-rope sailed through the air, wrapping around the giant's knee twice before the hook found its bite, burrowing into flesh and holding tight.

A thousand-thousand warnings rang in Berg's mind, words of his mother telling him to stay away from the people. Berg growled as the metal claws of a biting-rope etched a long scratch across his back, and the crowd responded with a growl of their own.

A sixth rope wound around his other wrist, then a seventh, and then Berg lost count as the townsfolk gained confidence and attacked him. At first, he tried not to fight, but fear overwhelmed the giant as the people began to shout and throw things at him. Hatred wrinkled the faces of the crowd, and Berg howled as the bite of the hooks pulling at his skin became too much.

He yanked his right arm, pulling six men to the ground. Two of them lost their grip, their ropes dangling from Berg's skin like dead snakes, but other men quickly took up their posts. Berg tugged with his other arm. The men tethered to his left were ready for the challenge, but they still found themselves no match for the strength of the young giant. Berg hefted eight of them in the air, then thumped them back to the cobblestone street.

Tears ran down Berg's cheeks. He tried to run toward the open gate, but more biting-ropes flew in the air, finding purchase around his neck, his forehead, his arms, his middle.

The crowd cheered as the young giant toppled to his knees. Men worked like choreographed soldiers, pulling Berg's muscular arms behind him and wrapping them tight against his back.

Berg looked into the crowd, hoping for help, but not a single friendly face returned his plea. Blood seeped from his wounds, red rivers running down his bare skin to the street below. Three men, full of bravado now that the giant was tied, launched themselves upon his back and rode him to the earth with a thump that shook the town like an earthquake.

Berg watched as the town celebrated his downfall. Somewhere church bells clanged, and the townsfolk held each other up and chanted a chorus that hurt Berg more than a thousand-thousand biting-ropes ever could.

Ünhold, Ünhold. Thief of all.
Greatly, slowly, watch him fall.
Ropes and daggers have him bound,
Safely fixed upon the ground.
Sing and dance and celebrate,
Ünhold, Ünhold, thee we hate.

ÜNHOLD!

The celebration continued into the night. A bonfire was built, and a goat was roasted. Mead flowed in the streets as the mighty giant hunters clinked together copper mugs and congratulated one another. Children climbed on Berg, their tiny feet dancing on his back, yet the young giant never uttered a word. Throughout the night he'd watched for Anya, but neither she nor the strange thin man with the curled mustache returned.

The party would have continued if it weren't for the blizzard. Cold wind coughed icy rain that quickly turned to snow, and, once again, Berg was left alone.

A blanket of snow covered his body throughout the night, burying Berg beneath a shroud of untouched white. Only his eyes and mouth remained uncovered as he continued to blink and breathe away the flakes as they fell. He was too sad to be lonely. He was too distressed to be tired. All Berg could do was lay as still as a stone upon the frozen street to keep from tightening the biting-ropes that bound him to the ground.

Before the night had fully fallen, he'd watched the townsfolk lower the iron-and-oak gate across the entrance of the city wall, where it remained fixed in place, locking him inside as if the tangle of biting-ropes were not enough. A church bell clanged ten times, and, one by one, the iron shutters were drawn closed and locked tight. A hush descended on the city.

The lonely night seemed frozen in time. Hours passed, and the snow continued to build. The city was perfectly still.

Then the gate rose to reveal a shadowy figure at the entrance. The gate closed again, slow and silent, but something had entered the city. Berg recognized the shape of him at once, for nothing he'd ever seen compared to the size and power of the ancient giant, Ünhold.

Berg's eyes watered as he watched the massive beast stalk into town. With fear pressing down on him, the young giant tried to think like a pile of snow, and he hoped it would be enough to hide him from the beast. Guilt surrounded him as he thought of all he'd taken from the old giant, and he was certain Ünhold had arrived to even the score.

But as the giant walked around the city, he seemed unaware of Berg. Ünhold sniffed at the chimneys of Eisenstadt, pulling stories from the smoke that leaked from inside. He stopped at one of the sleeping homes, and Berg saw something that made him burn with anger beneath the snow—Ünhold wore Berg's satchel over his shoulder. The satchel that had once belonged to Berg's mother.

Berg's heart ached as Ünhold reached into the leather pouch Berg had lost in the river. The beast brought out a pinch of star-blue-sand. He sprinkled the sand on the window ledge, blew it in through the shuttered window, and then crouched on his enormous haunches.

The iron windows creaked open, and a man Berg recognized as the beekeeper leaned out and dropped a copper bowl full of boiled potatoes directly into Ünhold's hands. The old giant dropped the bowl and potatoes into the stolen satchel, then rose to move to another home.

Time and again, Ünhold swapped star-blue-sand for food and treasure from the townsfolk, filling his satchel with everything from leather boots to bundles of onions and garlic, a treat the old giant liked too much to save, as he ate them all on the spot.

The snow continued to fall as Ünhold worked his way toward the center of town, but Berg had seen enough. Ünhold had stolen his mother's satchel, and now he was raiding the townsfolk. The old giant didn't need what he took; Berg had seen Ünhold's stash of food and riches.

Berg struggled against the ropes, trying to free himself from his web. He knew he was no match for the old giant, but now that anger had grabbed hold of Berg, he was ready to take the chance.

Ünhold turned his head and looked directly at Berg, and the young giant stopped fighting against the ropes, his anger swapped for fear as the beast's eyes locked with his. Ünhold crossed the courtyard on silent feet, a night-stalker's trait he and Berg shared. He stopped and looked down at Berg on the ground. He was so close the young giant could smell him. A deep rumble sounded from inside Ünhold's chest. The noise pushed Berg's fear to the surface, and he hollered with all his might, shouting the only word he knew would save him.

"Ünhold!"

The giant staggered back, his eyes wide with disbelief.

"Ünhold!" Berg's voice echoed through Eisenstadt, bouncing off the rock and iron walls.

The townsfolk began to wake, and people leaned out of windows, dressed in their nightclothes.

The old giant turned and ran, his wide feet slipping in the snow beneath him. He lowered his shoulder and headed toward the iron-and-oak gate.

Men spilled from their doors, hooked-ropes and pointed-sticks in their hands. Arrows were slung and ropes were tossed, but they did nothing to slow the beast.

Ünhold smashed through the gate with ease, tearing it from the rock wall and sending a shower of sparks and splinters of wood around him. The gargoyle wolf fell to the ground and spun around to face the charging townsfolk, his fire-breathing mouth and searing eyes warning them to stay back and live another day.

BOOK FOUR

WHERE WE LEARN
HOW A GIANT
EARNS HIS KEEP

THE MAYOR

Berg woke beneath a cloak of snow. He listened to the shuffling of feet approaching, a small crowd too timid to speak out loud and too terrified to come too close. A man cleared his throat, but the boy-giant remained rooted to the earth. Someone jabbed Berg's forehead with the blunt end of a wooden rod. Berg did not react. He was sore from his struggle with the biting-ropes and scared by what the people might do to him next. The crowd spoke in hushed whispers that pierced Berg's ears like daggers.

"He's dead."

"I hope so."

"Frozen."

"He wasn't dressed for a snowstorm."

"You can't freeze a giant. Be careful, Mayor. It's trying to fool you."

Berg heard careful steps, but he couldn't see a thing as he lay beneath his arctic cover. A shadow stopped in front of the giant, and he closed his eyes a second before the coarse, straw fingers of a broom swept the snow from his face. Berg felt every bristle, his skin raw and sensitive after a night beneath the storm.

He waited for the scrubbing to finish, then blinked his eyes open and peered at the gathering of curious townsfolk.

They surrounded him, holding on to one another to get a better look at the giant freshly birthed from the snow. With faces hidden behind shawls and scarves, they whispered secrets to one another and gawked at him with fear and excitement in their eyes. The man with the broom stood closest. He was nearly as thin as the broomstick he held, and he wore a jacket as black as crows' wings. A pair of spectacles perched on his long nose.

Berg looked for a flash of warm, red hair in the crowd, but she was nowhere to be seen.

The narrow man crouched next to Berg and smiled, not a trace of fear upon his face. The crowd warned him to stay back, calling him "Mayor," which he wore as both a title and a name.

"Are you cold, giant?" He waited for a reply, scratched his pointed nose, and then asked again. "You may speak. We all heard you last night. Don't be shy. Are you cold?"

"No," replied Berg.

The man turned to the crowd. "He said no. He is not cold." He announced it as if it were a great discovery, and the crowd chattered in response.

"Are you hungry?" the mayor asked, then leaned in to hear the answer. Berg smelled something sweet on the man's breath.

"Yes."

The mayor repeated that Berg was hungry, and the crowd reacted again, this time their voices louder and more excited than before.

The narrow man spoke quietly into Berg's ear, keeping his words from reaching the bystanders. "I am a reasonable man, giant, but I would be a fool to let you go. I know you mean no harm, but not everyone shares my . . . understanding. They fear you. Who can blame them, really? Some believe you are

Ünhold himself, but I know better. You are not like the other one. You are soft. You are simple."

Berg said nothing, but he knew the man was right. He was soft. He was simple.

"We captured you. It was easier than we thought. There is no fight in you, giant, I can see that clearly now."

Berg was embarrassed that he had no fight in him, but he knew the mayor was right once again.

"I think I know what you want. I think you want to stay in Eisenstadt. With me and my people. Is that correct? Do you want to stay in this fine city? To be one of us?"

Berg nodded slowly, his ear and cheek grinding into the icy ground.

The man smiled, showing a row of polished teeth as crooked as an old picket fence.

The townsfolk mumbled, unable to hear the words between Berg and the mayor, curious to the point of boiling over.

"Good," the mayor said, his black, curling mustache twitching. "I want you to stay too, but you will need to offer me a promise. Is that something you can do?"

Berg nodded again, doing his best to keep his gestures small, although the offer to stay caused his heart to leap in his chest.

The crowd began to ask questions of the mayor, but he held up a hand and hushed them.

"We have a place for you, giant, to sleep during the day. But if you stay, you must walk the iron walls of Eisenstadt every night. You must frighten away any unwelcome or undesirable traveler, be it giant or be it rat. Both have walked the streets of this fine city long enough. Is this agreeable? Do you still want to stay?"

Berg lay in the street, nearly frozen and fully trapped beneath the biting-ropes. His eyes filled with tears, and a wide smile he hoped the townsfolk would not take for a scowl formed upon his face. He began to breathe quickly, his large puffs of breath forming clouds of steam in the cold air. The offer to stay among the people was all he had hoped for. It was an answer to his longest and deepest desire.

He answered the mayor plainly, not wanting to miss the chance. "Yes, I will watch the city. I want to stay."

The mayor smiled, then winked at Berg. It was a gesture the boy-giant did not understand, but somehow it made him feel even colder as he lay beneath the snow. The mayor stood, showing his back to Berg. He held his arms out wide as if offering to embrace all the citizens of Eisenstadt.

The crowd hushed.

"Bring the chains. I have convinced the giant to stay."

THE IRON OF EISENSTADT

The people of Eisenstadt surrounded Berg as he was led through the iron-city. Townsfolk ran from their homes to join the parade. They had fixed his wrists with iron cuffs, so finely made they looked like blue-black jewelry made just for him.

Berg had seen iron before, but this was different. This iron was smoothed and oiled. Rubbed to a fine polish to reveal a color so deep it reminded the giant of a moonlit lake. While Berg didn't like being bound, he had to admit the cuffs were a work of art.

The enthusiasm of the city's children warmed Berg, and occasionally one of them would pry away from his mother's grip and jog beside the captured giant. Others would shout questions up to him or sprint to touch his ankles quickly, then run away.

Berg felt a tug to his left as the men directed him from the cobblestone street and down a muddy road. His body was pink from the snow and marked with sores that wept, yet he happily obeyed. Following his iron leads, Berg turned to see the barn that was to be his home.

A small group of men and women armed with pitchforks and biting-ropes and long pointed-sticks waited just outside the barn. He shivered as he remembered an ugly painting of an angry mob with weapons surrounding a giant, but he pushed away the dark thought, telling himself that this time was different. This time he was an invited guest. This time, though the people were still scared and armed with weapons, he would have a chance to show them who he really was. That he was kind. That he was like them.

Things quieted as the procession approached the barn. The doorway was twice as high as the tallest of the men and wide enough for them to enter four at a time. Berg felt the tug of the chains against his wrists, pulling him forward, and then he ducked his head and shoulders to make his way inside.

He hadn't noticed the chill wind outside that had brushed against his tender skin until he entered the quiet of the barn. It felt warm and inviting, and Berg was dizzy with gratitude.

The mayor entered last and worked his way through a crowd that watched in silence, their chatter tamed by the size of the giant in the barn. The mayor removed his black-glass spectacles and stood in front of the giant as the men bound the other ends of Berg's chains to two freshly cut timbers buried in the floor of the barn.

Berg looked around at the people of Eisenstadt.

"I don't need chains. I won't run."

The mayor smiled with his mouth, but his eyes were not amused, confusing Berg.

"This will provide some who worry with a bit of peace, that is all. I'm sure you understand," the mayor said. "You might have noticed by the iron walls and the ornate gargoyles scattered throughout that we are a city that takes great pride in our crafted metals. People travel for miles—days, even—to barter for our goods. Shields of brass, swords of steel, ropes capped with copper hooks." He motioned around the room. Berg noticed most of the men carried the ropes that had bound him the night before, and he swallowed hard as he remembered how the biting-ropes had yanked at his skin.

"But we are especially proud of our chains of iron. It is an honor to wear the chains of Eisenstadt. The set you wear now was created long ago to hold another giant that used to walk the roads of our city, terrorizing the peaceful people, but they were never put to use. Not until now. Not until you arrived. They are magnificent, wouldn't you agree?"

The crowd agreed, and Berg was encouraged by their approval, yet he still felt the chains were not necessary. He was not going to run.

The mayor looked over his shoulder as six women entered pushing wheel-barrows, half of which were piled high with boiled potatoes and the other half with raw turnips and field grasses.

"Go on. Deliver these fine goods to our guest," the mayor said.

The women looked nervous, but they did as they were told, wheeling the food up close to the young giant.

Berg smelled the food, and his stomach growled, a deep rumbling roar that made the people cringe and the mayor smile. Berg looked at the crowd with wonder. Only a day before, he had been on his own, and now he was being fed magnificent foods in the finest wheelbarrows he'd ever seen. He wanted to hold each and every one of the townsfolk in his arms and squeeze them to show his appreciation, but he knew better. Besides, it would be impossible with his arms chained to the massive poles.

"Go ahead, giant. Eat. Be our guest. I'm sure there is slack enough in the chains to feed yourself."

"Berg," the young giant said before he reached for the food.

"What was that, giant?" the mayor asked.

"Berg. It is my name—Berg."

The mayor laughed, and this time others joined in until the barn rattled with laughter. Berg heard his name flying through the barn like invisible birds, and he nearly laughed himself as he saw the joy on the faces of the townsfolk.

"I ask you, my people," the mayor said to the townsfolk as he pivoted around the room, "could there be a more fitting name?" He turned to face the giant again. "Berg is what we call the mountains that surround this valley. Bergen."

Berg smiled. He loved the mountains and was pleased to share their name.

"Have you another name, Berg? A surname, perhaps?"

The giant shook his head. He didn't know what a surname was. He'd been called other things, but he was only Berg.

"Well then, today we shall give you another. Wenig. Berg Wenig. Our Little Mountain."

The people of Eisenstadt cheered as they crowded in the barn. Then, old and young, woman and man, the people shared his name with each other, tasting it on their lips.

Berg felt something he hadn't felt in a hundred-hundred days. Berg Wenig felt accepted. Ever since his mother had gone, Berg had wanted to be welcomed in by the people. To be seen as one of them. To be called *little*. His thoughts turned to the days ahead of him, of living a simple life among the people of Eisenstadt. And while his body was still beaten and tired and his wrists were bound in chains of iron, for the first time in a long time Berg felt at peace.

He picked up a wheelbarrow of boiled potatoes and dumped them into his mouth and smiled wide to show his gratitude to the people of Eisenstadt.

To his people.

GESUNDHEIT

Voices chattered outside the walls of Berg's barn as he listened to the children giggle and tease. It was the finest sound he'd ever heard, and one he dared not interrupt.

"Wait until you see him. I swear he barely fits. They stuffed him in like a badger through a mousehole," a girl said.

"I can't believe I missed it," a second voice said, nearly as high-pitched as the first, yet it carried a gravelly quality that told Berg he was a boy.

"Scoot over. I can't see," said a third.

The rustling sound of children jostling to look between the slats of the barn thrilled Berg, and his mind bubbled with images of playing with the children, a dream he'd never allowed himself before.

"They chained him up good, but he said he didn't need the chains. The grown-ups all looked worried, even the guards, but he didn't scare me," the first voice bragged. "He even talked before they brought in the food, but once the food was there, the talking was over. That giant can sure eat a lot of food."

"More than Konrad?" a new voice asked, followed by more giggling.

"Almost," the first voice said. More giggles and a protest from the boy Berg guessed must be Konrad.

Berg wished he could free himself from the chains to get a peek at the boy who could eat as much as a giant.

Berg grinned as he listened to the children retell his story. He'd heard others talking about him in the past when he hid behind homes or beneath bridges in other towns, but this was new. These stories were full of joy. Full to the brim and ready to burst.

"Is he asleep? My dad said giants sleep during the day so they can lurk around at night," said the voice of another boy.

At first Berg wanted to correct the boy, but he knew the boy was right. He did travel around at night and sleep during the day. He wondered if that was something he should change. He would be less lonely if he was allowed to walk the city during the day.

"Come on; let's go around to the other side. There's a big knothole over there that'll give us a better look."

The talking stopped, but the young giant imagined the children walking on tiptoes, searching for a crack in the walls big enough for them to peer through. He wanted to speak to them, to invite them in, but Berg worried he'd scare them away.

The children kicked up dust as they struggled to get a look at the giant. Berg felt a sneeze coming, but being a boy of the forest, he took no efforts to conceal it. He jerked forward as he sneezed, rattling the chains that wrapped around his arms.

"Gesundheit!" yelled a girl, and then the children ran like spooked rabbits. They whooped and laughed as they left the barn behind, and Berg allowed himself to smile, pleased with how well the visit had gone. He'd listened to them talk. He'd seen them between the dark slats of the barn, and they'd looked at him without cringing. But best of all, they had found his sneeze funny, not frightening. In fact, he was certain they'd share the adventure with the other children of Eisenstadt, and Berg hoped he'd be able to delight them as well when they came back.

He slumped back down on the dry-dirt floor with a new goal in mind. One he knew was of the highest importance. He had a task to do.

Berg had to teach himself to sneeze at will.

WE WILL HAVE
NO FIGHT FROM YOU

en armed with heavy tools and biting-ropes marched inside the barn, waking Berg from a near-night snooze. He sat up and watched as they formed a semicircle around him, well out of his reach. A large bald man wearing thick clothes and a leather apron stepped forward and spoke with a staccato voice. "Bring the cloth and the bread."

Two more men entered, one carrying a few loaves of overcooked bread, and the other hefting a large piece of tan burlap over his shoulder.

The leather-clad man spoke as he walked toward Berg. "Tupen, Brooks, Markenson. Help Johansen with the drape. I can still see too much of this giant."

The guard's words were as cold and hard as iron. Tears threatened to escape from Berg's eyes. Crying had never seemed wrong to him before, but as he sat among the men, he somehow knew crying here would be wrong. Bad, even. He swallowed the tears back with the lump in his throat.

The four men unrolled the burlap, each taking a corner. A ragged hole had been cut in the middle of the heavy fabric.

"Duck your head and let them cover you, and we'll let you have some bread," the man ordered.

Berg did as he was told, bending his head toward the dry-dirt floor. The cloth rubbed against his ears and cheeks as the four men placed it around his neck, letting it drape over his shoulders and arms and along the chains that remained fixed to the poles.

"We are going to undo your chains now. We'll have no fight from you, or we'll fight back. Do you understand?"

Berg nodded. The scent of burning torches was strong, but the subtle smell of bread crept to his nose as well. Four men separated from the pack to unlock the chains attached to Berg. The iron cuffs remained, but they felt light in comparison to the weight of the heavy, dark chains.

The leather-clad man continued. "The mayor has instructions for you, giant." He removed an hourglass from beneath his apron. He inverted it, and sand began to trickle from the glass bulb at the top to the bottom. "You are to stay in this barn until this timepiece runs its course. Eat the bread while you wait." He nodded to the baker, and the old man tossed the burned loaves to the dirt.

"After this, you are to leave the barn and walk around the city wall. You will be the night watchman. You must not allow anyone to enter. The mayor said no giants, no men, no rats are to enter the city on your watch." The leather-clad man looked at him in disgust, obviously not pleased with the mayor's decision to let Berg stay in the town. "You must be back in the barn before sunrise. Do you understand?"

Berg nodded again. He was afraid of the leather-clad man but grateful that he had a task to do. He was to be the night-watch. He was to keep rats and men and other giants from entering the city. He fought back a smile as he thought of Anya, hoping that he'd be able to see her again beneath the moon and stars. She was no rat. She was not a man. And she was surely not a giant like him.

Nearly all the men left the barn, leaving Berg alone with the leather-clad man. He glared at Berg until the giant was filled with shame he didn't feel he had earned. He dropped his gaze to the dry-dirt in front of him and slowly began to cry.

"I don't like this, giant. I don't like letting you off those chains. Not one bit. Don't cross me. I'm not as kind as I appear."

The leather-clad man backed out of the barn, keeping his eyes on Berg as he faded into the night.

THE NIGHT-WATCH

Watching the sand trickle through the hourglass had been frustrating, but the obedient giant waited until every grain had spilled before he rushed from the barn. The night sky was crisp, and his feet crushed puddles of ice pooled on the empty streets. He owed the people of the iron-city a debt, a payment for the kindness they'd shown him.

But Berg couldn't get Anya off his mind. He rushed to the city gate, intending to do a quick run around the city to see if all was safe before looking for her, when he saw the fallen head of the gargoyle lying in the street. The pitted iron wolf snarled up at Berg, and he knew how he could repay the people.

The weight of the mighty gargoyle strained Berg's back as he held it in his arms, its carved edges digging into the sores on his body. The young giant grunted as he pushed the chunk of iron above his head and lowered it in place with a grinding thunk to its home above the gate. Berg and wolf stared at each other as the giant gasped to regain his breath. What he saw pleased him; he had done well—well enough to pay Anya a visit before he continued his task as night-watch.

Walking toward the mayor's house, he wondered if the girl actually wanted to see him again. She hadn't been to visit, but perhaps, he thought, she preferred to walk at night beneath the stars like he did.

It was dark inside the home, and he worried that Anya, sleeping behind iron-covered windows, wouldn't wake and see he was there. He wondered if she had decided he was too big to be her friend, if she was ashamed of him. He had nearly talked himself out of hope when he heard her voice below him.

"Hi, Shorty."

He looked down, and she smiled up.

"I am not short," he said.

Anya laughed so hard she had to cover her mouth with both hands to keep from waking the city. Berg watched and listened to her as her giggling tickled his ears once again.

"You are funny," she said between bursts of laughter.

Berg wished he knew what he had done to make her laugh because he'd like to do it again. He wasn't even entirely sure what *funny* was, but he liked how it made him feel.

"Do you want more candy?" Anya's eyebrows bounced up and down as if they were laughing with her.

"I would like more candy." He wiggled his brow up and down, trying to mimic her gesture. "But I don't have any sand."

"Too bad. Next time, then. But the mayor said you're the new night watchman. Would you like some help?"

Berg nodded and wiggled his eyebrows up and down again. Anya laughed, and Berg tried to smile.

"We've got to work on that smile," Anya said affectionately. She raised her arms and waved him to bend down. "Come on—give me a lift."

Berg lowered his hand, and she climbed aboard, and in a few minutes, the giant had carried her to the city wall. He placed her on top of the wall and leaned against it. Together, they looked out into the valley beyond the city. A light snow began to fall, and the clouds reached down to touch the earth.

Anya bundled her scarf tighter around her neck. She looked at his thin burlap frock. "Aren't you cold?"

"I don't get cold often."

"You're lucky." Anya shivered.

Berg was happy he had her along for his job as night-watch, but the questions in his mind were so strong he was unable to relax and enjoy the quiet night. He started with an easy one. A question not about himself.

"Why is the city so empty at night? In a city, there is always someone walking around."

"I walk around," Anya teased.

"Yes. But you are the only one."

"You walk around."

"It's my job to walk around. I am the night-watch." Berg stood a little straighter, proud of his new title.

Anya smiled again and gave Berg the answer he craved. "There is a curfew. One hour after sunset, everyone is to be inside their homes, doors bolted. Eisenstadt has a long history with unwelcome guests, and they only come at night."

"Other giants?" Berg asked.

"And thieves, and other things as well. That is if you believe all the things you hear," Anya replied.

The back of Berg's neck and his cheeks felt warm as he built up the courage to ask a more important question. The conversation lulled as he tried to pull the right words from the many that flew around inside his mind.

"Did you not want me to come back?" His words felt clumsy in his mouth.

"Of course I did, silly."

"Then why did you try to shoo me away?"

Anya's shoulders slumped, and she puffed a tiny cloud of steam from her nose. "It wasn't that I didn't want you back; it was that you came back during the day. The others . . . they don't see you like I do. I was afraid they would hurt you, and they did."

Berg rubbed his shoulder, massaging one of the many sore spots left behind by the biting-ropes.

"It was awful what they did to you, and I knew there was nothing I could to do stop them, so I tried to get you to leave."

"But you didn't stay."

"The mayor made me leave."

"He didn't stay either."

"No. But he watched. I'm sure of that."

"Did you watch?"

Anya shook her head.

Berg heard something crack in the woods far away, but he paid it no mind. He knew the sounds of the woods, and years of experience told him it was nothing more than a tree stretching in the night.

"Berg? Why do you stay here? Why don't you run away now that they have unchained you?"

"I like it here. They gave me this." Berg ran his hand down the burlap clothing covering his chest. "They let me sleep in the barn. They bring me food."

"But you could have almost all of that, plus all of this." Anya waved her hand toward the woods. "The sand could feed you, and sleeping in the barn is not all that great. I've tried."

"The sand doesn't always work, and the woods are lonely. I like being here with them." Berg paused. "I like being here with you."

"I like being here with you too." She looked at him and smiled. "And the sand only works at night. I think it has something to do with the moon and the stars."

Berg knew she was right. He felt foolish that he hadn't thought of it on his own. They sat in silence as more clouds floated down to earth, filling the city with fog and bringing a chill. Anya shivered again.

"Why do the people need the sand? Don't they dream without it?" Berg asked.

"These people have seen horrible things. Or at least they know the tales of horrible things. Without the sand, they dream of . . ." She trailed off, and Berg waited for her to finish. He wanted to know of the horrible things the people dreamed of. "Let's just say the sand gives them happy dreams."

"Do you need the sand to have nice dreams?"

"I've seen sad things in my life, but not many horrible or scary things. Sad things aren't all bad. I'm okay if I dream about sad things," Anya said.

Berg had seen horrible and scary things. He'd been chased by men with weapons and dogs with sharp teeth. He'd been called bad names and had rocks thrown at him. And although he hadn't slept much since the men of Eisenstadt had wrapped him in the biting-ropes, he worried he'd dream of them later.

But the young giant understood what Anya had said about sad things. He dreamed of his mother from time to time. The dreams he had about her always made him feel closer to her. Even if they were sad, he would never want to trade them for dreams about happy things.

"I should go," Anya said. "Will you take me back? I have something for you."

Berg nodded, then carried her back to the mayor's house, where he lifted her to her lofty window, then waited outside in the dark. She returned quickly with a smile and reached out her hand, the small vial she wore around her neck dangling from her fingers.

"Here. Take this," Anya said.

Berg could see a shimmer of the star-blue-sand in the bottom of the vial, glowing like it did in the cave. "But this is yours."

"I think you need it tonight more than me. You seem sad."

"But I'm not. I am very happy. I've never been so happy." Berg tried to smile again to prove his point.

"That smile." Anya laughed lightly. "We have got to fix that smile."

"What's wrong with my smile?" Berg covered his mouth with his hand, embarrassed at his broken smile.

"Never mind. Take the sand." She handed him the vial, then stepped back from her window. "Good night, Shorty. Sweet dreams."

He pinched the little vial of sand between his thumb and forefinger. He waved good night to Anya, then headed toward the city wall again.

Snow floated down around Berg as he slumped with his back against the city gate. He was feeling quite tired. He popped the cork off the vial and emptied it into his hand, and as the little blue tornado spun, Berg finally understood Anya's joke. He laughed to himself. She knew he wasn't short; everyone did, and that is why calling him Shorty was funny.

Perhaps, Berg thought, he could learn to be funny too.

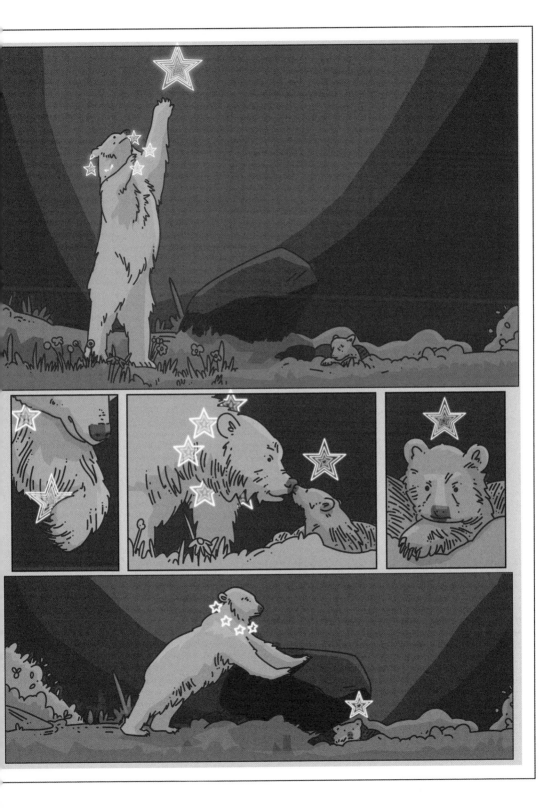

SMOOTH AS S!LK

Rocks make effective alarm clocks.

Berg's hand went to his forehead before he opened his eyes. The spot above his left eyebrow ached as he pressed against it, trying to convince it to stay put. He opened his eyes to see men approaching with their biting-ropes and angry faces covered with thick beards and knitted scarves.

Someone shouted, and ropes flew toward him. The men had surprising aim, wrapping his wrist, his forearm, his ankle, and his neck. Four copper snakes bit into his skin, holding tight and reopening old wounds that had just begun to heal.

"Get up, giant," the leather-clad man commanded, already dressed in his ironworker's apron and long gloves. The others shouted as well, barking harsh words like a pack of angry dogs.

Berg stood. He knew what he'd done wrong.

He opened his mouth to apologize when another rope swung around his right leg, wrapping tight and biting into the meat of his thigh. Berg used his free hand to unhook the rope. It wasn't meant as an act of defiance; it was simply a reaction to the pain, but the men panicked, and another volley of copper-headed hooks sailed through the air.

"Take him to his chains," the leather-clad man shouted, spittle spraying from his spiteful mouth. The ropes bit deep as the men pulled from every direction.

Berg stood firm, grimacing in pain.

The men pulled him forward, guiding him through the town as the people of Eisenstadt spilled to the streets or stared at him from behind barred windows.

Berg bowed his head and hunched over, both out of shame and with the hope of lessening the pressure on the ropes that clung to his face and neck. He could hear the people laughing at him, a sound that bore deep into his stomach like a hot spike of sorrow and dishonor.

He had done something bad. He had fallen asleep while on watch. He had only meant to close his eyes for a moment, but he had slept until the sun had risen, and, for all he knew, Ünhold could have entered the city as he slept. Berg had failed at night-watch.

"Stop! What are you doing?" a familiar voice shouted.

Berg saw the mayor through eyes veiled with tears. The commanding man wore a shiny robe of black and slippers lined in white rabbit fur. Berg noticed the mayor had taken time to wax his curling mustache before coming to his rescue.

"Stop at once!" he repeated, and the men obeyed.

Berg stood in the middle of the street, caught like the world's largest insect in an impossible web of ropes.

"Let him go. Do you not see what he has done?"

The men let go of the ropes. They uncoiled and fell around Berg's feet. The streets were full of curious townsfolk, and Berg looked for a flash of orange hair, but he knew Anya would not be seen.

The mayor marched right up to Berg and began working to free him from the ropes, reaching as high as he could to unbind the giant. New gashes criss-crossed old, and Berg winced as the skinny man tugged at the ropes. When he had done all he could, he spun around and addressed the guards.

"You should be ashamed of yourselves! Berg Wenig has done nothing to deserve this." The mayor looked directly at the leather-clad man, then pointed to the entrance to the city. "Look what he's done. He replaced the wolf watchman. It's no wonder he fell asleep. That would have taken ten of your strongest men and more planning and strength than I believe you're capable of."

The mayor walked away from Berg and the men who had attacked the giant with their biting-ropes. He addressed the crowd.

"He walked the city last night. Did he interrupt your sleep?" he asked a woman covered in a wool shawl the color of oatmeal. She dropped her head to study the street between her feet. "Was anything stolen from your home?" he asked another. "Did he welcome others like him into our midst? If you had no gate to protect you, wouldn't you still sleep comfortably in your homes, knowing our Berg Wenig was on watch?" He waited for a reply but was treated to silence in return.

Berg's guilt boiled inside him as the mayor continued to come to his defense. Berg knew he had not followed the mayor's command to return to the barn. He felt as if he did not deserve the praise the small man provided.

"Berg Wenig is our guest. We need him. Do you want him to hate us? Do you want him to leave?"

The mayor waited again for a reply that would never come. He turned to the battered giant. Small streams of blood trickled down Berg's skin.

"Come, Berg Wenig. Walk with me."

Berg and the mayor walked away, leaving the townsfolk behind. The young giant walked as slow as he could, but the mayor nearly had to jog to keep up.

Neither of them spoke until they turned off the cobblestone street and headed down the mud road toward the barn.

"They don't understand you like I do, Berg Wenig. I see you for your potential, not your past. I want to be your friend."

Berg couldn't believe his luck, and he didn't dare speak. The promise of having another friend seemed as fragile as thin ice, and he didn't want to shatter it with thick words and clumsy thoughts.

"Is that all right with you, Berg Wenig? That I want to be your friend?"

Berg nodded. It was the best he could do. He was unable to speak over the growing lump in his throat.

"Let's get inside where it is warm." The mayor opened the door to the barn, and Berg ducked and entered. "I hate to ask you to do this, Berg, but could you chain one of your hands? Knowing you are locked up will help them. Will comfort them."

Without protest, Berg slid an iron pin through his cuff, locking the chain in place and binding him to the pole once again.

"They don't see what I see inside of you, but they will soon," the mayor said.

"How will they see inside me?" Berg was confused, thinking there was something literally inside of him the mayor could see. Something broken but kind.

The mayor filled a bucket of water from a trough in the corner of the barn, then placed it next to the boy-giant. "We will show them together, you and I." The mayor removed his shiny robe and dipped it in the water. He lifted it from the bucket and wrung it out, then began to wash away the blood and dirt from Berg's feet.

Berg was too stunned to react, but the cool water and smooth cloth caused a chill to run down his spine, and he shivered, rattling the iron chain noisily. The mayor laughed but kept cleaning the blood from Berg's rough skin.

The young giant heard footsteps outside the barn and looked toward the door.

"They are coming to bring you food. And to bind your other hand, I suppose."

"Isn't one chain enough?"

"Not for them." The mayor dipped the silk robe back in the water and wrung it out again. "Will you help me, Berg Wenig? Will you help me show them how you can be of great use to them? How you can do something for them they could never do for themselves?"

Berg's mind seemed to lighten as he thought about helping the city. About helping the mayor. He began to think of the many things he could do with his great size that no one else could do. With a grateful heart, he answered the mayor.

"I will, for you, Mayor. You are my friend."

The mayor looked at him and winked as water dripped from his hands, leaving behind coffee-colored spots on the dusty floor. "And you are mine, Berg Wenig, and I am very fortunate indeed."

A BRIGHT NEW ANGER

It had been three days and two nights since the mayor had washed the giant in the barn, and in that time, Berg had performed his task of night-watch without fail.

Anya joined him every night, and they talked about the deep-wild-woods, warm fires, and hot meals. They talked about candy and summer nights and bright, shining stars. She hadn't been as direct as the mayor, but Berg thought that perhaps she was his friend as well. She'd even given him a copper shaker filled with pepper, a magic black dust that made him sneeze at will, a trick he hadn't had a chance to try but hoped he would soon.

There was no watchful-moon that night, and the full-night sky was black and dotted with a thousand-thousand stars. The men who freed him from his chains had not arrived on time. In fact, they were very late, which made Berg anxious and a little angry.

At first, he thought the noise outside the barn was the men coming to unbind him for his night-watch job, but as he listened to the noise, he became convinced it was something else. He smelled the beast—the bitter scent of age and sweat, smoke and filth, rot and ruin.

Pulling the chains to their farthest extent, the young giant leaned against the wall of the barn and peered through a crack between the slats. Shock overcame Berg as he saw Ünhold trudging toward the town, Berg's mother's satchel still looped over his muscular shoulder.

The town was vulnerable. The gate that Ünhold had crashed through upon their first meeting in Eisenstadt was still a gaping hole in the iron wall. Berg needed to be released from his chains to protect the city. If he remained bound, he would fail, but the guards still hadn't shown up, and he wondered if they had forgotten him all together.

From his limited view, Berg could tell the old one was heading directly toward town, and panic rushed through Berg as he thought of Anya waiting for him, alone and unprotected beneath the moon and stars. What if she mistook Ünhold for him?

Something new boiled inside him, and the chains at his sides rattled as his hands began to shake. A sound like crushing stones rolled through the barn as Berg ground his teeth. He sucked in a deep and powerful breath. He held the breath inside until it was hot, then pushed it through his wide nose, steamy air rushing across his chin and over his chest.

He felt in control, focused. Filled with a bright new anger. The blue-iron chains groaned as the young giant pulled them tight, creating a straight line between his wrists and the fresh timber poles that anchored him to the barn. Berg felt powerful and huge, and for once in his life, he liked it.

The muscles in his chest and back woke to the challenge, expanding beneath his burlap cloak until it was tight. The cuffs around his wrists cut into his skin, but his flesh did not give way first. The chains binding him to the timber poles burst as Berg pulled with all his might.

Freed, Berg shot through the barn, smashing the brittle wood, exploding an opening twice the size of the door that had once hung from rusty hinges.

Berg saw the tracks of the giant, a scar as wide as a river sweeping through the fresh, white snow. He ran, and the broken chains clanged down the street behind him. Ünhold's path led into town, working its way between the homes in a zigzag pattern. Berg raced down the alley, sliding on the icy cobblestone streets.

The open courtyard seemed to welcome him as he arrived. He entered, breathing deep and fast and angry. He looked through falling snow to the opposite side of the courtyard.

Ünhold was hunched over, less than a stone's throw away. His square head hung between his rounded shoulders, stooped with old age, yet still he towered over Berg. His hand was stuffed in the satchel, and Berg knew his fingers were touching the star-blue-sand.

Massive clouds of steam pulsed from Berg's flared nostrils, his gaping mouth. He was ready to confront the ancient giant, ready to fight if needed to protect the people of Eisenstadt.

To his left, he heard an angry mob of men, their work boots drumming against the street. The copper heads of the biting-ropes gleamed as they swung, catching the orange glow of the mob's torches.

Berg stood between the mob and Ünhold. The old giant hunkered in the street, unafraid, unaware of the hurt the men could bring with their biting-ropes, their stabbing words, their fear-fueled hatred.

He looked into the eyes of Ünhold, and the bright anger washed away from Berg, replaced with something new. Something sorrowful. Something protective and profound. Something somehow ageless and important.

He turned to Ünhold, the ancient giant, and whispered a single word.

"Run."

BOOK FIVE

WHERE WE LEARN
OF TALLEST-TREE AND
LEATHER SATCHELS

A NEW TASK

After watching Ünhold run away, the men of Eisenstadt had surrounded Berg. They hadn't exactly thanked him, but they hadn't wrapped him in their biting-ropes either, which Berg was grateful for.

After finishing his night on watch, he returned to his barn, the broken chains dragging behind him on the dry-dirt floor. Cold followed him through the opening of the barn, now a jagged mouth of splintered wood. He watched the storm through the hole in the barn and felt heavy and sad, knowing he'd caused the damage in his haste to chase Ünhold into the night.

His mind flowed like river water, his thoughts swirling, never ending, and impossible to stop. Now that the townsfolk knew their chains could not hold him, Berg worried he'd lose their trust, assuming he had ever earned it. But most of all, he thought of the old giant.

He thought of Ünhold, his ancient body being beaten and wrestled to the frozen ground by angry men. It hadn't happened, yet the image of the giant entangled in the biting-ropes was as vivid in Berg's mind as any memory he'd ever held.

The river of bad thoughts kept him awake as he'd patrolled Eisenstadt through the night and as near-dawn passed and as near-day arrived. Now, eyes closed, he sat with the barn-mice and straw-bugs and an old owl that had taken up residency long before Berg had been invited in. He listened to his bedfellows squeak and scurry and hoot, and he knew that even his anxious thoughts were no match for the sleep that was creeping up on him.

Berg was tired. Berg was bleary. Berg was spent.

He had nearly given in to the welcoming tug of sleep when he heard his name. Berg opened his eyes and saw the gangly figure of the mayor standing in the open mouth of the barn.

"Berg Wenig. Did I catch you napping, my friend?" He walked into the barn carrying a burlap sack over his shoulder, and Berg could smell the food. "You had an interesting night. I heard you scared away the giant, Ünhold. We are once again in your debt, Berg Wenig."

Berg held up his hands. "But I broke the chains." He looked over the mayor's shoulder. "I broke the barn."

"Barns can be repaired. Chains can be mended. But for now you must eat. I have a new job for you. That is, if you are not too weary from last night's duties. Duties you accomplished valiantly, I must say."

The sleep that had nearly claimed Berg moments before left the barn. He was excited for a new task, and as he studied the narrow face of the mayor, he was overwhelmed by his continued charity. "I am not too tired."

The mayor smiled, his sharp cheeks pushing up to forge lines at the corners of his eyes. "You will be after this, I'm afraid." He slid the sack of food from his back and placed it in Berg's lap. "Eat up, Berg Wenig. You'll need your strength."

Berg rolled back the top of the sack, feeling the warmth of freshly cooked food soak into him. A hundred-hundred boiled eggs covered a bed of steamed carrots and potatoes. "Thank you." He popped two eggs in his mouth and swallowed them whole, feeling the globes glide down his throat.

The mayor nodded, then spoke. "There is a tree that grows in the forest beyond our fair city, a mountain ash as old as the earth itself. A proud and noble tree, it stands four times the size of any of its neighbors. It would take an army of men standing hand to hand to surround the tree. It truly is a sight to behold."

Berg finished the eggs and was pleased to find a roast turkey hidden beneath the vegetables. He looked up at the mayor, who had paused his tale, and smiled.

The mayor nodded. "Go ahead—the food is all yours."

Berg chuckled to himself; he couldn't help it. He'd been given food before, but nothing this fine. He raised his eyebrows like he'd seen Anya do, hoping the gesture would convey the gratitude he felt.

The mayor simply smiled, then continued. "I need you to bring this tree back to me. Do you think you could do that?"

"How will I find it?" said Berg through a mouthful of turkey and potatoes.

"It's to the west."

"Where is west?" Berg said.

"West isn't a where. West is a direction, a heading." The mayor paused, and Berg tilted his head in confusion. "West is where the sun goes down."

"Ahh," Berg said, "I understand." And he did.

"It should be easy to find. There is no mistaking this tree. It stands out among all the others, much like you do, my friend. But I'm surprised you haven't asked me how you are to fell the tree."

Berg didn't understand what *fell* meant, and the mayor answered his unspoken question.

"To fell a tree means to cut it down. To topple it over," the mayor explained.

Images flew through Berg's mind. Walking through the forest, comforted by the tall trees that surrounded him. Sheltering beneath the toppled trees, their wide bodies protecting him as he slept. He loved the trees in the forest very much.

He wondered if Anya would like to come with him to see this tree, for she had told him she too loved the trees and the way they whispered with the wind. Berg swallowed the thought with a mouthful of turkey, knowing the mayor would never let her join him.

"I have felled many trees before. Pushed them over, roots and all," the giant said with pride.

"Yes, but not this tree. This tree will not be pushed over, not even by one as strong as you. This tree must be cut." The mayor grinned, wrinkles sprouting upon his sun-tanned face. He turned his head toward the door and whistled.

Three men entered through the demolished side of the barn, carrying a massive ax in their arms. The sight of the giant-sized tool filled Berg with joy, and he yearned to feel its weight and oiled wood in his hands.

"It's beautiful. I want to hold it." He didn't mean to speak, but the words were too honest to be held in his mouth.

"Of course you do. And hold it you shall," said the mayor. "But not yet. I'm afraid these men don't trust you as I do. You'll need to wait for us to leave. And then the ax is yours."

The mayor gestured to the men, and they stepped forward, placing the ax on the ground.

Berg could not believe how his life had changed since he had entered Eisenstadt. He felt as if he would drown in gratitude, smothered by the imbalance of how much they gave him compared to his list of failures as night-watch. He felt a great strength grow within him as he focused on felling the giant tree. It was a task only he could do. Something he could do for them.

"I am ready to go. I am ready to fell Tallest-Tree and bring it back."

"Don't you want to finish your food first?"

Berg had forgotten about the food. He looked at the bag in his lap; a few vegetables and half the turkey remained. "I'll take it with me."

"Very well then," the mayor said. "Bring forth your hands."

While sitting on the floor in the barn, Berg extended his hands to the mayor. A few links of broken chains hung from each wrist, tightly bound to the cuffs. The mayor pulled out a long key from inside his jacket. It was made of silver and nearly as long as the mayor's arm. He unbound the giant from the cuffs, letting them fall to the floor with a clang.

Berg was once again humbled by the kindness and trust the mayor was showing him.

"With your great stride and unending strength, it should be no more than a day's walk for you, perhaps two."

Berg nodded. "To west," he said as he stared at the ax resting just beyond his reach.

"To *the* west," the mayor corrected. "We'll be preparing for your return. We'll host a feast in your honor and ours." The mayor nodded at the three men, who ran from the barn as if it were burning. "Until we meet again, Berg Wenig."

Berg waited until the mayor was out of sight before making his way to the ax. Kneeling, he traced a rough finger down its wooden body. It was nearly six feet in length, and its metal head felt heavy, solid, as he lifted it tenderly, balancing it in his wide hands. He gripped the handle and swung the ax through the air. He yearned to feel the ax bite into Tallest-Tree.

The young giant's head thumped against the rafters as he stood, and he wondered how the barn had shrunk since he had moved in. At first the rafters had been a foot above his head, perhaps two, but he had more important things to think about than a shrinking barn.

Slinging the nearly empty sack of food over his shoulder, Berg said goodbye to the barn-mice and the straw-bugs and the owl, then hurried, unattached and free, with his new ax out into the cold. The sun blazed in the sky, melting away the snow.

It was near-day, and his shadow stretched out in front of him, urging Berg to follow it west, toward his new task. Toward Tallest-Tree.

VANTAGE

It had taken longer than the mayor had promised. For nearly a week, Berg walked west, napping and following the path of the sun in the day, dozing and then following watchful-moon at night. But by the end of the fifth day, he arrived.

The sun was a deep orange when Berg crested a rocky ridge overlooking the deep-wild-woods below and a thick spread of tall pines and firs and mountain ash. The trees were black, the highest of their leaves catching the orange of the setting sun, but one tree stood above them all.

Tallest-Tree—a giant among its peers. Berg had never seen its equal. It stretched so high it tore a rift in a fire-colored cloud.

For a moment, Berg forgot his task and simply admired Tallest-Tree and the shadow it shared with the canyon below. The remaining warmth of the sun welcomed Berg as his eyes feasted on the sight below him. He wished he could share it with Anya. He thought of her then, as the sun began to dip away, knowing that soon she would be watching for him beneath the moon and stars.

He had wanted to tell her he was leaving, but there had been no time before he left on the mayor's task.

The young giant had saved the ax's first bite, knowing that such a precious gift must be used wisely, but he could wait no more. He ran down the mountain, laughing, loving the feel of branches grabbing at him as he passed. The spicy scent of evergreens filled his nose, and forest mulch smashed between his toes as he tore through the woods toward Tallest-Tree.

By the time Berg reached the tree, purple shadows owned the forest floor and only a glimmer of warmth remained from the sun. Berg lifted the ax, the sharp edge of polished steel smiling and begging him to let it taste the pulp of Tallest-Tree. He swung the mighty tool in the air, feeling it tug as if it wanted to continue spinning though the forest forever.

The moon, its face nearly hidden, peeked at him through branches black in the night, and Berg spoke, his voice sounding hollow and odd to him in the forest.

"You don't fit here, Tallest-Tree. The others struggle to grow in your shadow."

The tree didn't answer—trees never do—but Berg could feel its understanding as the wind rustled its leaves. The tree agreed.

"I will take you with me. I'll find you a place to fit. A place where they already know your name, Tallest-Tree."

Berg stepped back, wound up, and let his ax taste wood.

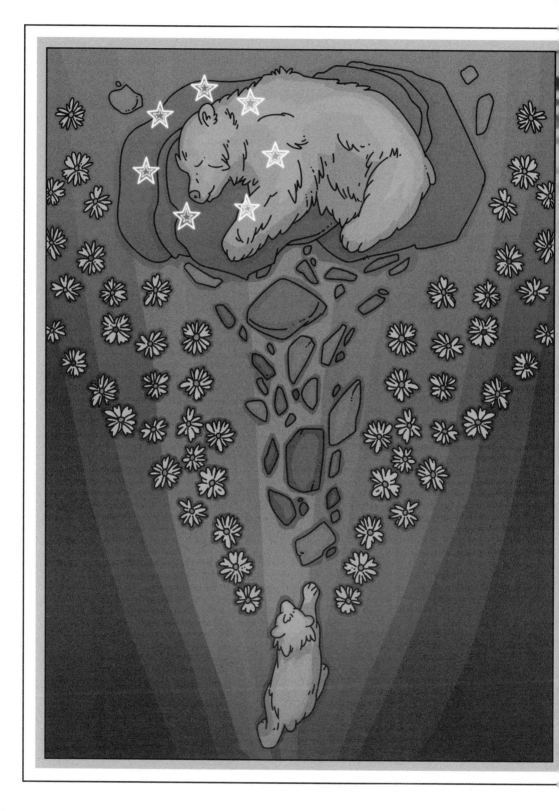

THE FELLING

The sky wept throughout the night, and the rain turned to ice as Berg slept, covering him in a glaze of frost. He rolled his neck in a wide circle, feeling his night of chopping at the tree deep within his shoulders.

His memories were filled with sorrow, brought on by the dream of the two bears.

Berg rose and turned to look at the tree. Tucked in the cream-colored gash opened by the ax was a small pile of food. The young giant moved closer. He sniffed at it, and found nothing out of the ordinary, except for the fact that it was there in the first place. Berg stepped away from the tree and peered through the deep-wild-woods that surrounded him. He studied the ground around the tree, and was not surprised to see the wide footprints of a giant pressed into the damp earth.

Berg followed the footprints into the forest, but they disappeared as the ground turned to shale at the base of a rocky hill.

He knew Ünhold had given him the food, but he didn't know why. He knew the old giant was a thief. He knew he scared the people of the iron-city. He knew by the bones in his cave that the beast was a skilled hunter.

But he was beginning to think that, like him, Ünhold was misunderstood. Berg had so many questions he'd like to ask the beast, but he was still afraid of him, even though Ünhold had helped him on more than one occasion.

"Are you there?" Berg shouted into the deep-wild-woods. Birds and forest critters skittered to safety from miles around at the booming of his call. "Giant. Are you there?"

Berg waited for a reply, but nothing returned. He walked back to the food he'd been given and ate his fill of apples, gourds, and salty strips of dried meat. He was grateful for the food, but as he looked at the scar he'd opened in the tree the night before, other emotions surfaced.

A sunbeam broke free from the dense forest to highlight the wound. Tallest-Tree had nearly been cut in two. Painful gouges were carved into the yellow-white belly of the tree, and sap dripped from the edge of the scar, weeping from under the tree's black hide. Berg looked up into the tree's branches, wide arms outstretched, and he felt the weight of what he had done.

Sorrow swelled in the young giant. He swallowed to wet the lump in his throat, hoping it would melt away before it brought tears, but it was no use. As Berg considered the weakened tree, tears poured down his cheeks. His breath came out in puffs and returned in gasps, not giving him the air he required. As his head swam, he leaned against the tree, buckled over with sadness and regret.

The task the mayor had given him seemed simple at first, but standing buried to his calves in woodchips, Berg knew he had no right to take the tree down. He had done it to please the mayor. To please the people of Eisenstadt. But he had underestimated the cost of the task. The difficulty. The brutality.

He placed his massive hands against Tallest-Tree, trying to soothe, trying to atone, but it was too late. The scar in the tree was too deep. If he could go back to the day before and leave Tallest-Tree untouched, he would. But hoping for that was as foolish as trying to reassemble the woodchips and place them back inside the gash he'd cut. He had gone too far to turn back now.

He wished with all his might there was another way. But Berg knew felling the tree, as wrong as it seemed to him now, was what he was expected to do. It wasn't just what the people of Eisenstadt required of him; it was that they allowed him to do it. By giving him the task and making him the ax, they were inviting him to be part of them. To be one of them.

But there was one among the townsfolk whom he knew would not approve, and he did his best to push her freckled face and bright-orange hair from his mind's eye. He and Anya had talked about the forest; their love for all things in the deep-wild-woods was something they shared.

Berg buried the shame he felt beneath his promise to complete the task. He hid thoughts of Anya behind closed eyes, and he pushed with all his might to bring down the mighty tree. His feet burrowed into the cold earth, and his back and legs flexed, but the tree barely swayed against his force.

Berg grabbed his ax, then slammed it into the tree, releasing a chunk of mountain ash the size of a leather-bound book. Again and again he swung as the sun crossed the sky, traveling from other-west to west. At last, Berg dropped the ax. The blade that had once bit with anger had been reduced to something as dull and tired as he was. The scar in the tree reached two-thirds into the massive trunk, and Berg decided to push again.

He placed his blistered hands against Tallest-Tree, pushing with all that remained in him to bring it down, but the stubborn tree refused to fall. Berg had no tears left. He closed his eyes. He was ready to fail again. Berg was ready to walk away from the task—and away from Eisenstadt forever. His heart wrenched with the thought of not being able to return to the first home he'd ever had. He tried to not think of Anya, but it was impossible.

He had given up when he felt the tree move. He opened his eyes to see Ünhold standing beside him, his giant paws pushing against Tallest-Tree. Berg shot away, falling to the ground and scooting backward, distancing himself from the old giant. But as he sat and looked up, he knew Ünhold was helping, perhaps repaying Berg for telling him to run from the mob in the city not long ago.

Ünhold looked old as earth, but his massive arms testified to his great strength as he added his weight to Tallest-Tree. Berg stood and joined him, pushing again, knowing his strength was but a shadow compared to what Ünhold could offer.

The tree cracked with a snap that woke those that slept in the deep-wild-woods, and then it toppled to the earth with a boom. Tallest-Tree was no more.

There was no celebration as Berg waited for the dust to settle. The tree lay on the ground, silent and still. Ünhold cleared a spot for himself among the woodchips, then sat with his back against the stump. Berg watched as the old giant opened the satchel by unwinding a length of once-red thread from around a deer-bone button. He pulled out a large roasted squash and two round loaves of bread and placed them on the ground. He nodded for Berg to join him. And, although he was still afraid of the old giant, Berg was too disheartened to disagree.

QUESTIONS UNANSWERED

Without the aid of Ünhold, Berg would not have been able to heft the fallen tree with its many branches through the deep-wild-woods. As the sun crossed the sky, they worked their way through the thick trees, across a river, over and through hills and valleys.

The day was eternal, but as they rested at the summit of a treeless hill, they were treated to a golden fall sunset. The old giant pulled a pipe fashioned from the leg bone of a moose from the seemingly endless satchel. Acrid plumes of smoke floated through the air, and Berg found the courage to speak.

"Do they call you Ünhold?" he asked, but the old giant didn't reply. Berg knew the answer, so he started again.

"Why did you help me? You pulled me from the river. You bound my wounds in the cave. And now you're helping me with this tree. Why?" Berg asked.

Ünhold's face glowed red as he drew upon his pipe, but again he offered no response.

"Do you speak? Can you hear me?"

Ünhold held the smoke in his puffed-out cheeks, then tilted his head toward Berg. He looked directly into Berg's eyes, then let the smoke flow from his nostrils where it mingled with his yellow-white mustache and beard.

"You can hear me. Can you speak?" Berg asked, reversing the questions but getting a similar result.

The old giant sighed, then let his shoulders slump. Berg watched the giant rub his hand on the chocolate-colored fur of his leggings. Berg did the same, rubbing his palms on the rough burlap throw he wore.

"Do you make your own clothes?" Berg gave the old giant plenty of time to respond.

Berg went to the fire and rolled out a large pumpkin Ünhold had produced earlier. Its orange skin now black, its flesh steaming and tender. Berg pulled the squash in two, then held out half to Ünhold. The ancient giant took his share, and Berg thought he saw him nod slightly, but it might have been a hiccup.

"I've always been in the forest. First with her, then by myself." Berg paused, not sure he was ready to talk about his mother yet. Ünhold sat on the trunk of Tallest-Tree across the fire from him, but Berg could tell he had heard him. He knew he must carry on.

"I remember her eyes the most. Mother's eyes and voice, I guess." Berg hadn't said her name aloud since she'd gone, and he felt both relieved and tortured as her name floated between them.

"She was kind, and we made each other laugh. And she was tall. Much taller than me." Berg looked up from the large squash he was toying with more than eating. "Taller than you too, I think, but it was too long ago to remember for sure."

"We lived in other-west, where the sun wakes up. The trees are shorter there, but the deep-wild-woods are much older. We ate wild grass and mushrooms and birds' eggs and rabbits, and once in a while, she'd find a sheep. She would cook it beneath the earth in a deep pit covered with hot rocks." Berg smiled at the memory, its return to him as warm as blood. "I was never hungry, not with her. Not with Mother.

"One night she woke me. She smelled like fear. She grabbed our things, my bag filled with my forest-jewels, the snow-cold-clothes she'd made from the skins of the sheep and rabbits we'd eaten. She led me through the woods as fast as my feet could run. I could hear men and their barking dogs behind us. She was fast, faster than me with my small legs and heavy bag. She told me to leave it, but I refused. The treasures were all I had."

Berg slumped closer to the fire, craving its warmth as the story he told began to chill him. The tale had lived inside him like a seed, but now the seed had sprung, and it needed air to grow. He knew he must finish.

"She pushed me up a tall mountain covered with sharp rocks. She'd been there before. She'd been everywhere. She found a cave, and we tried to squeeze inside, but it wasn't big enough for the two of us. She pushed me inside, then smiled at me and told me to wait until she returned. I begged to go with her. I didn't want to be left alone."

Ünhold emptied the remainder of his pipe in the fire, then stood, slipping the moose-bone-pipe into the satchel. Berg felt as if the old giant did not want to hear the story, but it was too late. The story must be heard.

"She wore a satchel with red thread and a deer-bone button. The same one you wear now. She opened the satchel and removed a pinch of sand. Star-blue-sand. She kissed me and told me she'd be back. She blew the sand in my face, and I never saw her again. She was gone, and all she had left behind was her satchel."

Ünhold stood at the edge of the fire's light, his shadow flickering around him as if it would take flight and leave on its own.

Berg stood and found great courage growing inside him, courage sprouting from the story-seed he'd kept inside for nearly half his life.

He was no longer afraid of Ünhold the Giant.

"The men caught her and brought her down. They sang songs about how she fought them. The songs still ring in my head today. It was my fault she died. If I had been smaller we both could have fit in the cave. We both could have hidden from the men and their awful dogs. She led them away and left me behind. Alone. And the only thing she left me was the satchel you're wearing now.

"I want it back, Ünhold. Although you wear the bag, it is more mine than yours."

Ünhold seemed to shrink at Berg's words. He let a massive breath flow slowly from his tired body. He turned away from Berg, away from the fire, and then, in a single motion, the ancient giant spun and tossed a handful of star-blue-sand into the fire.

A funnel of blue flames blazed into the air. Heat shoved Berg back, and he covered his face with the crook of his arm as the fire died down to what it had been before. His eyes adjusted, but only the night surrounded him.

Berg was once again alone.

HOMECOMING

Berg didn't wait for the morning sun. After Ünhold left him alone on the top of the hill with Tallest-Tree, the young giant was too upset to sleep. He wondered how he would ever get Tallest-Tree back on his own, but then watchful-moon showed him the way.

At the bottom of the hill, a silver ribbon of river water wound through the valley. He had followed the river from Eisenstadt, and he knew if he could get the tree to her waters, she'd help carry it home.

Though he was angry and sad at the way Ünhold had left him, he was grateful the old giant had helped him lug the log to the top of the hill. Berg heaved one end of Tallest-Tree to the side of the hill, then went to the other, wider end. He pushed with all his might, and the loose shale beneath the log shifted and slipped until, with a great crash and crunch, Tallest-Tree began to roll down the mountain.

The mammoth log tumbled through anything in its path, smashing smaller trees like twigs and tossing boulders in the air. Branches larger than most of the trees it passed by broke from Tallest-Tree, leaving a wake of debris and destruction that looked like a jagged scar on the face of the hill.

While luck wasn't something Berg was used to, he took it gladly as Tallest-Tree bullied its way to the river.

Berg rushed down the hill after it, not wanting it to float away without him. By the time he arrived at the river, there was no worry of that. Tallest-Tree was waiting for him on the edge of the rushing water. Once again, Berg felt guilty for felling the tree as it rested, lifeless, its limbs hewn short and stubby by the violent tumble Tallest-Tree had just endured.

With a great swing, he buried the head of his ax in Tallest-Tree, then walked waist deep into the cool water, steering the tree through the eddies and swirls in the slow-moving waters. While the river was a great aid, and at times did all the work, Berg found himself digging out shallow areas in the river and removing debris at a near constant pace.

It took more than a week for Berg to return to the valley that held the city of iron. Ünhold hadn't returned since Berg had asked for his mother's satchel, leaving the young giant to walk and wade alone as he floated the massive tree down the river.

When he arrived home, Berg wedged one end of the tree against the bank of the river, then used his strength and the flow of the powerful waters to drive the tree to the shallow riverbank. After wading from the river himself, Berg wrapped his hands around two stubby yet sturdy branches, broken and jagged from Tallest-Tree's journey, and he yanked the tree forward with all his might. His wide feet left deep divots in the muddy bank as he dragged Tallest-Tree out of the river.

Even in the light of near-day, Berg could see the town had changed. He had been gone for nearly two weeks, and in his absence, the busy men and women of Eisenstadt had built a grand structure outside the city wall. Fifty or so wooden poles were arranged in a wide circle surrounding a metal framework. What was once a field of shallow grass had been raked and tamped down flat.

Berg's eyes opened wide as he slowly turned his head to take in what the industrious men and women had built, amazed at their craftsmanship as well as their ability to work together to make something larger than themselves in such a short time.

He left the tree where it was, half in and half out of the river. He fell to the ground, his heavy backside landing with a thud. He had been tired before, but this was new to him. He was spent; he had nothing left to give. He rolled to his side, slamming his cheek and shoulder to the ground alongside Tallest-Tree. With a weary heart and blurry eyes, he looked at the tree. Her once-grand branches had been crushed down to rough nubs in the journey, and the white wood of her insides had turned brown, tarnished by the muddy water of the slow-moving river.

But it was the ax that bothered him most.

It stood proud at an unnatural angle that seemed to taunt the giant. He was ashamed of what he had done—deeply ashamed. And the ax was a reminder of the sins he'd committed in the deep-wild-woods. Berg stood, his strength nearly sapped, and went to the ax. He pried it from the tree as the tears he'd spilled throughout his journey returned.

Dragging the ax behind him, the blade leaving a furrow in the earth, Berg made his way back to the soft mud of the riverbank. Then, with his wide hands, he dug a grave for the ax. He placed it in the bottom of the hole, then wept as he buried the ax beneath rocks and mud.

As he returned from the river, covered in mud, the unmistakable clip of shod hooves took his attention in the near-day hour. He turned toward the noise to see the mayor approaching.

He was dressed in his usual finery, a suit the color of storm clouds and a top hat of purest black with boots and gloves to match. The white mule he rode stopped, and the mayor patted its neck to calm its nerves at being in the presence of the giant.

"I finished my task," Berg said.

The mayor's smile seemed fancier than his attire. He straightened in the saddle and looked at the massive tree. "I see. I bet you're all the hungrier for it. Come, let us get you cleaned and rested. The townsfolk will want to see you. They have been planning your return feast since you left."

Berg was pleased to see the mayor again and to be so near his barn where he hoped to tumble into a deep sleep, but he couldn't hide the shame he felt at felling the magnificent tree.

The mayor followed his gaze and said, "It will be fine right where it is. We can take it from here. Come."

Berg observed the iron structure, the broad stage, the poles arranged in a circle around them. "What is all this?"

"Ah, that is the home of a giant. Berg Wenig, this is your reward. A place for you to call your own."

Berg tried to smile and thank the mayor, but he was too tired.

"Come. Follow me," the mayor said, then he pulled his reins to the right and spun the mule around. He spoke over his shoulder as he led the way. "Welcome home, Berg Wenig. Welcome home."

BOOK SIX

WHERE WE LEARN OF
FRIENDSHIP AND
LIES BUILT ON TRUTHS

LEMON DROPS

Berg had no idea how long he'd slept. A day, perhaps two. But it hadn't been the restful sleep he'd enjoyed in the wild-woods. Now that he was back in Eisenstadt he was mindful of how quiet the town was at night. No swishing of trees as the night-wind stirred, no scurrying of night-critters in the dark. Even the old owl that lived in the barn left at night to make his hootings and huntings in the forest that bordered the iron-city.

In contrast, the day brought noise. People chattering, the hammering of metal being stretched across an anvil, the barking of town-dogs. The woods during the day were quiet as the sun plodded across the sky.

He sat up and realized the structure just outside the city wall wasn't all the people of Eisenstadt had built while he was gone. The iron chains he had broken had been mended, and they were attached to two iron poles buried deep in the floor of his barn, replacing the timbers that were once there. As he slept, the people had bravely placed the cuffs upon his wrists, and the ends of his chains were again fixed firmly in place.

He was a captive, locked in, and he felt shame and sorrow because of it. He knew he had done what was asked of him by bringing back Tallest-Tree, but he also knew he had done a great and horrible thing. While he didn't think the chains were necessary, he understood why the people had locked him up this time. He was capable of bad as well as good, and he thought his iron bindings were justice.

With a heavy heart and body still demanding rest, Berg listened to the townsfolk working on the new structure, his future home, hammering and shouting and driving teams of mules. The sounds were too strong for him to be tempted by sleep, so Berg decided he'd wake and watch the people work. Perhaps they'd even allow him to help.

He opened his eyes and saw Anya sitting in the loft above him.

"You sure do sleep a lot. I brought you something."

She held out a red-and-white-striped sack that Berg recognized at once. It was just like the one she'd helped him gather from Bartle Brickle's Sweetshop on the first night they'd met.

The heaviness of sleep vanished at the sight of the girl and her bag of treats. He hadn't expected to see her during the day, and the welcome surprise of finding her in his loft filled him with joy. Standing, he used his wide fingers to comb bits of straw out of his wild hair.

Anya's tongue poked out of the corner of her mouth while she dug inside the bag; then she smiled and extended her hand. Berg lifted his to meet hers, and she dropped four sugary lemon drops into his palm.

"Go on. They're for you. Don't be shy."

He tossed the lemon drops in his mouth and rolled them around on his tongue. His mouth filled with a bright flavor that made him instantly happy. He savored it as long as he could, which wasn't long enough, a few seconds at most. Then he crunched the golden-pebble treats and swallowed them.

"They taste like the sun looks," Berg said.

Anya found one for herself and popped it in her mouth. "Oooh, you're right."

Berg was happy she agreed with his description of the lemon drops, and he was thinking how he could ask for more when she began to speak.

"I wasn't spying on you, you know. This was kind of my barn first. I've been hiding here for years and years."

"Why do you hide in this barn?"

"Because the mayor would never look for me here. Especially now that you've moved in."

Berg couldn't imagine why anyone would hide from the mayor. In fact, he would be happy if the mayor and Anya were both with him all the time. "Why would you hide from the mayor?"

"Everyone needs to be alone sometimes." She shrugged and searched through the candy sack again. "You were gone for a long time."

"Yes," Berg agreed.

"Why did you bring back that tree?"

"Because the mayor asked me to."

"Did you cut it down?"

Berg nodded, then felt shame's shadow cover him again. Anya didn't ask any more questions about the tree, which suited Berg just fine. His stomach growled, and he gawked at it, then covered it with his giant hands. He glanced at Anya, and she laughed, the sound making Berg think of a rock skipping on a lake.

"You're hungry?"

"I am always hungry," Berg said. He tried to smile, and she wrinkled her nose and squinted her eyes.

"Did I do something wrong?" the young giant asked, feeling his cheeks flush. As he stood in the barn, he missed the free feeling they shared when they spoke at night, nothing hiding between them. It felt different now, and worry filled his mind. He wished the good feeling would return, but he didn't know to find it.

"No, no. But we've got to fix that smile of yours."

The iron chains rattled as Berg left one hand on his stomach and covered his mouth with the other, not wanting to feel a fool or show Anya his broken smile.

"Wait. Don't cover it up. It's actually great. It's a bit scary at first, but now that I really see you, it's kind of sweet. Like you've never seen yourself smile before."

Berg didn't know what to say, but he wasn't about to smile again until he could fix it. The peaceful feeling they'd shared beneath the moon and stars seemed further away than ever, and his shoulders slumped as he felt it slipping away.

"I'm sorry. I didn't mean to upset you. It's nice. Well, it could be. Here, one minute." Anya scooted forward in the loft, her scrawny legs dangling off the edge. "Come closer."

Berg shuffled over as far as the chains would allow. He had to look up to see her eye to eye.

"Hey. I'm taller than you," she said, inching closer to the edge. "How about that. Little Anya taller than Berg, the boy-giant."

Berg felt his knees weaken, worried she might fall like a baby bird from a nest.

"All right then, give us a smile."

The giant tried to smile, and Anya winced. "Okay, okay. Watch closely."

Anya smiled. Everything lifted, not just the corners of her mouth. Her cheeks, her eyes, even her tiny pink ears rose. "See, it takes your whole face. Pretend like your mouth is trying to push your eyes up over your head."

Berg tried, and she shared her rock-skipping-on-a-lake laugh with him again. Berg's face drooped.

"Sorry, not quite so much. And how about not showing your teeth? That might help."

"I don't want to smile anymore."

"Why not?" Anya asked.

Berg had no answer, or at least not one he could describe. Anya was so bright and nice that it made him feel dull in comparison. He looked down at his bare feet.

"Wait. I have an idea." She fumbled through the treat bag, then unrolled her hand and showed it to Berg. Five golden lemon drops teetered on her palm. "Here. Take these. Think of them as smiling pills."

Berg didn't know what smiling pills were, but he wanted the candy very much. His mouth watered, and he sniffed the air, trying to steal a hint of their bright flavor.

Anya grinned. "It's nearly there already."

"What is?" Berg asked.

"Your smile. I think we've found your weakness, Shorty."

Berg couldn't stop looking at the lemon drops resting on Anya's hand, but as he heard her call him by his funny name, the easy feeling between them returned.

"Go on. Before I change my mind."

Berg lifted his hand, and Anya passed the hard candy to the giant. What was a handful for her nearly disappeared in Berg's oversized palm. He popped the treats in his mouth, and immediately knew that five lemon drops were better than four.

"Now close your eyes and try again."

Berg obeyed. With his eyes closed, he focused on the tangy flavor of the lemon drops. He thought of Anya, his delightful, treat-sharing friend. He thought of the wonderful mayor and the people of Eisenstadt who had welcomed him into their lives and given him the barn. He thought of the new home they were building for him, and Berg smiled. He could feel the joy upon his face, his cheeks pushing up against the bottoms of his closed eyes. He even felt his huge ears lift the tiniest bit.

"There it is," Anya said, a voice from above. "And it's a good one, Shorty. That's a champion smile if ever I've seen one."

Berg opened his eyes and looked at her sitting in the straw with streaks of sunlight sneaking in between the slats of the barn. He kept the smile upon his face. He liked how it felt.

They sat together in the barn, smiling and listening to the clanking of the men building the iron structure outside of town. Then Anya tucked the bag of candy in her lap, and her expression changed.

"They've been telling stories about you, Berg."

"Who has?"

"The townsfolk. Everyone, I guess," she said.

Berg continued to smile. He loved hearing that the people were talking about him. Telling stories of how he had protected the town and returned with Tallest-Tree.

"Even you?" he asked Anya.

"No. Not me."

Berg was saddened. He'd hoped Anya would have joined in the storytelling.

"The mayor? Has he been telling stories?" Berg asked.

"Yes. Him most of all."

Berg smiled again, but Anya's face was serious in response. The young giant read the worried look on her face, and he thought of another type of story. Stories like he'd heard about Ünhold. Stories of fear and hate.

"What kind of stories?" he asked, not really wanting to know the answer, but realizing that was why Anya had come to find him in the barn.

Anya paused, her legs swinging back and forth.

"They won't let anyone come see you, Berg. There are men with swords who wait nearby, and they won't let anyone near the barn."

"But you're here. And the mayor—he comes often."

"The mayor does what he wants, and I have always been good at sneaking."

She delayed again, and Berg waited.

"After you left, there was talk that you had broken your chains to join Ünhold. There was talk you had escaped and that the men had chased you away before you . . . well, before anything bad happened."

"I don't understand."

Anya continued. "The mayor said that he sent three men after you. Three trackers. Men who could follow a fish in a raging river if they needed to, but those men never returned. The mayor said that he would go after them himself. He returned the next day to tell us he'd found their bones and there was no way of telling which of the two giants had done them in."

Berg couldn't believe what he was hearing. He was sure it was all a big mistake, and that Anya's story would turn happy again if he let her finish.

"Then a week later, you returned with that huge tree. The mayor said it was something you offered him as an apology for the bad things you'd done. The mayor said he tricked you into coming to the barn where he tucked you away and surrounded you with guards so you could not leave again. He said you promised to help us build the tent, to build your stage."

Berg shook his head and took a step back. Deep furrows wrinkled his brow, and he felt tired again, tired and frustrated by what Anya had said. "No! Not all of that happened, but some of it did. I did break the chains. I did bring back the tree. He did ask me to come back to the barn. But I didn't kill anyone. I would never do that."

"The best lies are always half-truths, Berg."

To the young giant, Anya words had always been soothing and delightful, but the things she spoke to him in the barn burned in his belly. He wanted to believe what his little friend told him, but he also trusted the mayor. How could they both be right?

Placing his head against the barn wall, Berg spied through a crack. Two guards stood before the entrance of his shelter: one held a pointed-stick with a bright silver top, while another one carried one of the biting-ropes, letting it swing lazily in the cold. Part of him wondered why the mayor surrounded him with guards, but as he looked at the once-broken chains now strong around his wrists, the larger part of him understood.

"It is not the mayor's fault, Anya. It is mine."

"What is your fault?"

"It is wrong for him to tell lies about me, but the mayor is right to lock me up." As he spoke, tears filled his eyes, and sorrow puddled in his heart.

"I'm not sure which is worse," Anya said.

"I am not like the others. I am both protector and threat; I know that now. How else would your people sleep? I must be guarded. I must be locked up." Berg heard the creaking of old wood, and he turned as Anya climbed down a wooden ladder.

She walked to him, as brave as a forest fire, and looked up into his dark eyes, her hands clasped behind her back.

"I worry for you, Berg, my giant friend." She held out the red-and-white-striped sack. Berg hesitated, but she nodded for him to take it. "If you knew what was best for you, you'd run from this place and never return."

"But I am happy here," Berg said with tears rolling down his cheeks.

The young giant could see that his little friend was sad, perhaps as sad as he was. He tried to smile to convince her that everything would be fine. That everything would be good.

"I'd better go. He'll start wondering where I am soon. Goodbye, Shorty." She passed Berg a half smile of her own, then headed toward the jagged opening of the barn.

Berg didn't want Anya to leave, but he was unsure of how to convince her to stay. He glanced around and saw she had left her red-and-white-striped sack of goodies. He pinched it between his fingers and called to her, "Anya. You left this."

Pausing, she twisted a half turn toward him. "You keep it. I'm not in the mood for sweets."

Berg realized he wasn't either.

"Will you come see me again?" Berg asked. "Will I see you as I walk as the night-watch?"

"Perhaps and perhaps," she said in her most grown-up voice.

"Perhaps and perhaps," Berg echoed. As he watched her sneak from the barn, he hoped that *perhaps* meant *yes*.

THE MAYOR RETURNS

The confident gait of the mayor was easy for Berg to recognize. The narrow man made his way to the barn, then swung a bag of food from his shoulder to the floor. He looked up at the young giant.

"You've grown again, my friend," he said with a wink and a nod.

Berg tried to respond in kind, but smiling was difficult after his talk with Anya.

"You look worried, Berg Wenig. Is everything all right?"

Berg nodded.

The mayor pushed the food toward Berg, who took it and examined the bag. Turnips, raw and covered with bits of the field where they'd been harvested. He was grateful but couldn't help thinking of the roast turkey from before. And the lemon drops. As he looked at his supper in the burlap sack, his mind swam with memories of star-blue-sand, Ünhold's cave of wonders, and little Anya and her bright hair and rock-skipping-on-a-lake laugh. Berg nearly forgot the mayor was in the barn until he spoke.

"Once again, I'll say you seem at odds, Berg Wenig. Are you quite sure you're feeling all right?"

Berg nodded. "I am fine." But the warnings Anya spoke filled his head with questions he dared not ask. The trackers who had been killed. The story told of Tallest-Tree being brought back as an apology. The guards surrounding the barn. All these thoughts confused Berg because he liked the mayor. But the lies he told about Berg worried him. They worried him a great deal.

"Is it the iron poles that hold your chains? I'm sorry, my friend, but you know they are necessary now. The people—they are cowards. They don't know you like I do," the mayor said.

His words sounded buttery in his mouth, and Berg wondered if they were lies built on half-truths. And although being locked in the barn bothered him, it wasn't what was weighing him down.

"Is it the men who surround the barn?" the mayor asked.

"A bit. I don't like the biting-ropes."

The mayor's face contorted as he searched for the right response. "I'm not sure those are necessary, but the men are there at my request. Precautions must be made for the sake of my people. Images must be upheld."

"Images?" Berg asked.

"It is important, for now at least, that the people of Eisenstadt keep a certain . . . How should I say this?" The mayor looked up into the rafters to where the old owl slept. His face folded in on itself as if he were squinting to read the right words etched in the air. "They must keep a certain distance from you. It's important they hold inside their minds a similitude of who you are now to who you were then."

"I don't understand."

"You will. All in good time, my Little Mountain. All in good time."

Berg held the bag of soiled turnips in the air, then twisted the burlap flap shut and tucked the food away for later. The weight of the stories filled with lies felt heavy on Berg's mind, and once again the mayor came to his aid, helping him out by offering him another task.

"But for now, my Berg Wenig, we could use a bit of help. A little muscle if you will."

"Outside of the barn?" Berg asked. He hadn't realized how much he craved the fresh air beyond his wooden walls until that moment. Now he felt if he didn't get a deep breath of crisp air soon, he would be smothered beneath the weight of the barn.

"Yes. We need help building your new home."

"Will the men with the biting-ropes be there?"

"I'm afraid so, but don't worry. I will be by your side at all times."

That promise provided less comfort than it had before, and Berg still wished the guards would stay behind. He wanted to show the mayor and the townsfolk that he did not need to be surrounded by the men and their weapons. He thought his need to show that he was good was as strong as it could get, yet the desire had deepened as he learned of the stories the mayor had been telling the people. Promising himself that he'd ask the mayor later about why he had told the lies, he stood and readied himself to leave the barn.

"I will help."

The grin the mayor had been hiding sprung forth. Berg noticed at once that his eyes were not playing along with his smile.

"Excellent, my friend. I knew you'd feel this way. Show me your hand, Berg Wenig," the mayor said.

Berg extended his arms toward him.

As if by magic, the mayor produced the long silver key again, and Berg wondered how he had kept it secret. He hadn't noticed it beneath the mayor's shiny cloak, and he wondered what other things the mayor might be hiding from him inside his cloak.

The mayor slid the key into the lock on the chain holding Berg's right wrist and gave it a twist. The mayor unlocked his left chain, and Berg began to massage and rub his wrists as he stared at the chains below him, lying in the dust of the barn like snakes.

"Thank you," Berg said, grateful the mayor was showing him so much trust.

"My pleasure, my friend. I've removed your chains so you can help us with the pole, but we will not be alone, as I have said."

"I understand," Berg said.

"Good. Come then, Berg Wenig. Let us place the pole. The very tree you carried from the woods."

THE CENTER MAST POLE

The bones of the iron structure emerged as Berg followed the mayor through the fog. It had grown since Berg had last laid eyes upon it. A few men were working in the near-day hours, orange sparks zinging from their hammers as they pounded bolts into the metal spans.

The mayor led Berg to the center of the clearing. A wide hole had been dug at the foot of the giant tree, twice as deep as any man. The bark and stubby limbs of Tallest-Tree had been removed, and the buttery-white flesh beneath had been smoothed and shaped. A series of chains were fixed to the top of the tree, evenly spaced and expertly welded into place around an iron cuff that seemed familiar to Berg. Without realizing it, Berg began to rub his wrists.

The sight of the imprisoned pole disheartened the young giant. He had caused this. He and Ünhold had brought down Tallest-Tree.

"This is the center mast. The very heart of our tent. Of *your* tent, Berg Wenig." As the mayor spoke, the men with biting-ropes moved closer. The hammering stopped, and men climbed down from ladders to join in. They formed a circle around the young giant.

"But we cannot lift the center mast on our own. This is why I have brought you here, Berg Wenig. To help the men place the pole."

"Would you like me to lift it? Would you like me to put it in the hole?"

"We can help you. We can pull on the chains and lighten your load," the mayor said. Some of the strongest men dropped their weapons and began to stretch and pop their knuckles.

"No. I will place the pole."

"But . . ." the mayor started.

Berg looked at him, his eyes loaded with tears ready to fall. He needed to do this alone. He needed to replant the tree in the hole, and something in the way he looked at the mayor expressed this in a manner he never could have done with words.

The mayor waved his arms, and the guards stepped back.

Berg walked to the top of the tree, the growing circle of onlookers moving with him. It was his first time without the iron cuffs and chains since the day the people had tied him to the ground and sung songs as he fell.

Kneeling at the tree's crown, he caressed the lifeless bone of Tallest-Tree. Inside his mind he told the tree he was sorry, afraid that if he spoke aloud, he would lose his battle with the tears. Berg was through letting the townsfolk watch him cry. He'd shared enough tears with them already.

The log teetered as Berg heaved it in the air, and the crowd around him oo-hed. His arms and back and legs flexed as he muscled the log forward. And although his body nearly buckled beneath the weight of his task, the only sound was Berg's heavy breathing and the scratching of the center mast he pushed toward the hole in the ground.

The tree slammed into the hole, shaking the earth. Berg huffed for breath. He had hoped replanting what remained of Tallest-Tree would ease his guilt, but the act only seemed to drive his cares deeper inside until he felt he would crumble. He used his wide feet to push dirt into the hole, tucking the tree into its new home with care.

The fog thinned, and Berg looked at the faces of the townsfolk. They watched in awe. For a moment, Berg expected them to cheer, but they were not impressed by his deed; they were terrified by his show of strength. He tried to smile at them, but even as the smile formed, he knew it was not right. His brow had not lifted as Anya's had. He bared his teeth, another lesson learned and forgotten, as he stood anxious to gain their favor.

The people winced and began to retreat. Only Anya remained behind, standing closer to Berg than most, but still well behind the guards with their biting-ropes and long-pointed-sticks at the ready. She watched Berg as he stood, surrounded. He watched her, and he could clearly see streaks on her dirty face where tears had washed her freckles clean. She wiped her jaw with the back of her hand, then turned and walked toward the city without a single word.

FAIR TRADE INDEED

Without a moon overhead to mark the time, Berg had no idea how long he'd dozed. He had stayed throughout the day and night to help the townsfolk raise the tent. As he worked, Berg's mind played the image of Anya crying over and over in his mind, juggling what had caused her pain until he'd convinced himself of the worst. She cried because she was disappointed in Berg. She had cried because she was ashamed of Berg. She wept because she could no longer see him as a friend.

With thoughts too painful to bear, Berg had buried himself in work. He labored alongside the men until he could not think or lift any more; then he'd simply sat with his back against the center mast pole and slept.

The guards lay on the cold ground around him, snoring and groaning, unwilling to leave their appointed posts, but unable to stay awake either. He was about to wake them and tell them to go home to their toasty beds when the weathered silhouette of Ünhold working his way between the homes in Eisenstadt caught his eye.

Berg hadn't seen Ünhold since the ancient giant had escaped him on the mountaintop. With silence belying his size, Berg crept from the sleeping guards and made his way toward the city of iron.

The city gate was drawn when Berg arrived, and a new lock was in place, making it impossible for him to lift the wall and enter Eisenstadt. He walked around the city, searching for a weakness in the iron wall and wondering how the old giant had gotten inside. There was none, but as he looked ahead, he saw star-blue-sand glittering against the face of the fortified wall. He smiled to himself, knowing at once how the giant had entered.

The handholds were nearly invisible, but the sand Ünhold left behind showed Berg where to grasp to scale the wall. He worked his large fingers into a crack, then found a small ridge barely wide enough for his bare toes to grip. He continued climbing until he reached the top, and in a flash, he'd climbed back down the other side, safely tucked inside Eisenstadt.

Without the aid of the moon the city looked dipped in ink. Berg's feet brushed frost from the cobblestone street as he moved between the homes, searching for the ancient giant.

Metal clinked against stone somewhere out of sight, and Berg squeezed into an alley. He was grateful for the fog, the only thing in town large enough to hide him.

The scraping of metal against cobblestone continued, growing closer to Berg as he hid from whatever brought the noise. He froze, holding his breath and willing his heart to beat softly as he watched the ancient giant pass the alley, dragging behind him the ax Berg had buried. What was once fear turned to anger, and for a moment, Berg considered rushing out into the street and taking it back. But the old giant halted, leaving the city as hushed as before, and Berg decided to watch and see what Ünhold would do next.

Soon the young giant heard the whisper of a spinning pinch of star-blue-sand. He was close enough to smell the giant. Berg leaned out from his hiding spot between two buildings and watched as Ünhold bent nearly in two to align with the second-story window.

As he watched the old giant, Berg realized how long it had been since he'd used the sand himself. He remembered the mayor gifting him a loaf of bread and a small pile of apples for the sand he'd offered. He remembered being caught by Anya as she snuck up on him in the street. He remembered how he felt when Anya had shown him how to use the sand without opening a window, and how she had given him most of the bag of candies from the sweetshop.

Berg knew it was his task, his duty, to keep the people of Eisenstadt safe, and he wanted to protect them. He wanted to protect Anya. But try as he might, sitting in the cold alley a few feet from Ünhold, he could see no reason to scare the giant away. Ünhold was a thief. His satchel and the ax proved that, but Berg had never seen the old giant harm the townsfolk of Eisenstadt. Because of Anya, Berg understood the value of the sand and dreams, and as he watched the giant blow the star-blue-sand through the window of the little home, he saw that it was a fair trade for whatever bit of food or scattered treasures the sleeping people inside were willing to offer.

Much to Berg's surprise, nobody sleepwalked from the home to provide Ünhold with food or treasure. Instead Berg heard something he'd never expected. The sound was nearly silent, but as the young giant tuned his ears, he heard the old giant singing into the window.

The melody was cavernous yet sweet. It was slow and lulling, and the words that reached Berg's ears reminded him of the dreams he'd had, full of playful bears and birds and important warnings of wolves. The song did not build or lift; it simply was, until it ended.

The old giant reached into the satchel and placed something small on the windowsill, and then Ünhold turned and walked away without payment for the dreams or the song he'd left behind.

Berg could hardly believe what he had seen as he listened to the scraping of the ax Ünhold dragged along the street. He lingered in the alleyway until the city settled into silence again, and then he stepped to the home Ünhold had visited. He crouched to look into the small second-story window.

Behind the glass, an old woman curled on a bed no bigger than Berg's foot. The old woman's nose twitched, and she pulled a wrinkled hand from beneath her covers to brush a few grains of star-blue-sand from her cheeks. She was content, happy even.

Berg noticed then that Ünhold had left something behind for him as well. Six lemon drops, lined up in a neat row on the ledge. A sign that Ünhold knew he was being watched.

THE LEGEND OF
ÜNHOLD THE GIANT

og turned to snow as Berg walked the city. Since the near encounter at
the old woman's window there had been no sign of Ünhold, but he was
present in Berg's thoughts as he patrolled as night-watch.

Occasionally he caught glimpses of guards lurking around corners and
behind half-closed shutters. He realized the curfew that normally locked the
people inside had been lifted for those tasked with watching the young giant.
Berg was being watched, and it stole the joy he usually felt as night-watch, leaving only hollowness inside.

He saw her then, wrapped in a shawl at the end of a narrow road, the ladder and wagon she pulled behind her giving Anya an unmistakable silhouette.
Thoughts of her crying as he placed the center mast pole froze Berg where he
stood. He wanted to run to her and ask her to join him in his task, but Berg
was certain the young girl was too disappointed in him to continue to be his
friend. He raised his hands and waved to her as wide snowflakes tumbled down
between them, and she returned his wave with one of her own. It wasn't a smile,
but it was enough. Berg approached, leaving colossal tracks behind him.

"Hello, Shorty."

"Hello." Sunshine parted the sorrow in his heart as those two small words told him that he was wrong, that she still wanted to be his friend.

"Take me to your barn. It's chilly out tonight."

Anya tucked her wagon and ladder into an alleyway, and then Berg hid her in his hands and carried her to his home. A few guards were waiting outside his barn, huddled around a small fire.

The barn was warm inside, away from the falling snow, and Anya shed her shawl as she sat on a bale of straw.

"Will the guards stay all night?" Berg asked.

"Yes."

"In the snow?"

"Yes. When the mayor says guard, the men guard. Snow doesn't change a thing."

The guards who had watched him in the city joined the others at the fire. Berg stooped over to look out the hole in the barn.

"Tomorrow the canvas for the tent will arrive. I heard my uncle speaking about it earlier. It will take most of the town to cover the tent. He said it will come on twelve wagons pulled buy a hundred mules."

"I can help," Berg said.

"Only if he asks you, and I'm guessing he won't. There are others coming soon, visitors. He won't want them to see you."

"Is he afraid I will scare them?"

"Something like that," Anya said.

Berg wasn't sure what she meant. He asked another question. "Why are the others coming?"

"Didn't he tell you? My uncle. The mayor. Didn't he tell you anything?"

"Are they here to see the tent? To see the center mast?"

Anya shook her head.

"Are they here to see me?" Berg asked.

Anya fiddled with the hem of her shawl, rubbing the frayed ends between her small, pink fingers.

"I see," Berg said, understanding why she didn't want to tell him that they were here to see him. They sat for a while, lost in their own imaginations, and then Berg thought of another question he wanted to ask the girl who knew everything.

"What do you know of Ünhold? What do you know of the other giant?"

"What do you mean?"

"Why are the townsfolk scared of him?"

"He is why we have the curfew and the iron shutters. He is why they built the wall around the city."

Berg sat in silence and waited for her to continue. He knew there was more to the story, and he wanted every word.

"There are stories, you know," Anya continued. "Stories told to children to make them behave. Tales told to keep them from walking alone in the woods. Stories to keep us from sneaking around at night while everyone is asleep."

"But they are only stories. Stories cannot hurt you."

"Ah, Berg. Stories *can* hurt you, but stories can also keep you safe," Anya said.

Berg didn't understand.

"My great-grandfather was born in this city more than one hundred years ago. At that time, Eisenstadt was already surrounded by the iron wall. His great-grandfather was born in the city as well, two hundred years ago, and still, the city was protected by the wall. His great-grandfather was also born here, three hundred years ago, but he had no wall to keep him safe, and the stories come from him.

"Back then, the people lived with fear. At first, Ünhold sat at the edge of the woods and watched, but even his presence struck terror in the hearts of most of the townsfolk. But soon, he'd walk the city at night. People draped their windows, blocking the giant's shadow as he passed by their homes. This went on for a while, until the fields the farmers had planted were ready to harvest.

"Ünhold became bold. The giant helped himself to the crops. The stories say he'd sit in a field of pumpkins during the hot summer and eat his fill while the people tried to scare him away, hitting him with rocks and jabbing at him with sharpened sticks. He would swat them away like flies and continue his meal.

"Eventually Ünhold made himself comfortable in town, sleeping in the middle of the street during the day. Nobody could convince him to leave. A lot of people gave up, sneaking away at night with their families and whatever they could pack on their backs, leaving their homes empty. Those that stayed hid in their homes, terrified of the giant.

"Ünhold took what he wanted. He wasn't like you, Shorty. He had no manners. He'd smash things, break through windows and doors and take what he could. He continued to live off the people throughout the winter, pushing those who stayed behind to their weakest point. But in the spring, the people had had enough."

"What happened?" Berg was wrapped in Anya's story, more captive to it than the iron bands that had once clung to his wrists.

"My many-great-grandfather went for help. He rode away and returned with an army of men. The people of Eisenstadt were not a warlike people; they had no way to fight the giant, but the men who returned with my ancestor did. They called themselves the Hunters, and they were determined to take down the giant.

"The Hunters and my many-great-grandfather drove Ünhold from the city. Chased him away, up into the mountains. The people of Eisenstadt began building the iron wall that very day, and three years later, the wall was nearly complete. But none of the Hunters had been seen since."

"But your many-great-grandfather. What about him?"

"He was the only one to return, nearly five years from the day he'd left with the Hunters. He was a strong man when he left, or so the story goes, but as he limped into the city, he was nothing more than a skeleton wrapped in sun-rashed skin.

"He told the people of Eisenstadt that the giant had led them far away, over rock mountains and through dense forests. For nearly four years, he and the Hunters pursued Ünhold, but they only had glimpses of him as he led them away from home. Eventually the giant learned to walk without a trail, and the men were lost. Then one by one, Ünhold stalked them down, stealing away one soldier a night, returning his bones in his sleeping spot the following morning as a reminder."

"This story is sad," Berg said.

"It's a legend. I'm not sure how much of it is true."

"Some of it. I'm sure of that. Some of it feels true."

"Yes," Anya said.

It was so quiet in the barn that Berg could hear the snow falling on the roof. They sat for a while, absorbing the legend, and then Anya finished the story.

"As far as most people knew, Ünhold never returned, but they lived lives filled with lies, for the giant had never left. He returned every night and traded the dream-sand for goods from the city. The people would often talk about how clumsy they were to have lost a favorite candleholder or remark on how much bread they had eaten the day before.

"Ünhold's legend formed who we are. Everyone must be locked inside their homes when the sun goes down, and nobody is allowed to walk the streets at night. We live inside a fortress made of iron. We garden and farm within the walls, never trusting our crops to go unprotected at night. We have taught ourselves to be a warlike people, learning how to make and wield swords and pikes."

"And biting-ropes," Berg said.

"Yes. And biting-ropes," Anya said. "Then, just as winter broke, a giant returned, and the people, my people, treated him as if *he* were the monster, Ünhold."

Berg nodded, understanding more about the people than he ever had. He understood the importance of his task. The people didn't want his river-shined-rocks and bird-skulls. The people didn't even want the star-blue-sand. The people of Eisenstadt wanted to be safe. To be protected.

"But they were wrong, Berg. And while there are those who would like us to think that you are as bad as Ünhold, worse even, I know who you really are.

"You are kind," she said as she stood. "You are young and full of hope, and, if you don't mind me saying it, you are a bit of a fool."

Berg nodded. He was a bit of a fool. He knew that now.

"You need to leave. You should burst from this barn and run. They chased Ünhold because he ran, but if you don't run there's no telling what they'll do."

"I can't," Berg said.

"Why not?"

"Because I am here to help. I can protect you from Ünhold."

"But who will protect you?"

"Protect me from what? I am not in danger."

"That's just it. You *are* in danger." Anya wrapped herself in her shawl, then crossed the one-roomed barn to peer out the jagged opening. "As will I be if I don't return home before the sun comes up."

"I'll take you," Berg offered.

Anya let out a deep sigh as she looked at the army of guards who surrounded the barn. "It is too late for that," she said. "Good night, Berg."

"Good night, Anya."

She offered one last plea before sneaking out into the snow. "You don't know my uncle. He is not what he seems. You should run, Shorty. Run while you still can. Run before he makes you his."

UNHEARD WORDS

After finishing his work, Berg was cuffed once again. He slept fitfully as he dreamed of giants smashing homes and terrifying the people of his city.

The next morning arrived with great noise as a small crowd of men hammered a canvas drape over the hole Berg had smashed in the barn. Berg's view of the outside was limited to what he could see between the cracks in the walls now. And even those were difficult to reach while fixed to the blue-iron beams. He had been locked inside all day, alone with his thoughts and fears, listening to the rolling crunch of horse-drawn wagons bringing visitors to the city and watching the men outside march and puff up their chests to show their great strength.

But as full-night approached, the guards huddled close, surrounding a fire they'd made, soaking in its heat and light. They exchanged stories and guttural laughs, but the distance between Berg and the guards swallowed up their words.

Waves of visitors trekked into town through the snow, their faces shielded with wide-brimmed hats and woolen scarves, their hands covered in thick mittens. As the dark arrived, Berg could no longer see the carts through the cracks in his wall, but the roll and scrape of their wooden wheels on the icy street continued as the guards told their stories around the fire.

A slender figure approached the circle of men, and the guards snapped to attention, starched straight by the presence of the mayor. A flour sack containing Berg's supper was slung over his shoulder. The commanding man spoke in hushed tones, but his eyes burned with anger.

Berg heard nothing, but he understood. The mayor was angry at the men for hunkering around the fire instead of encircling the barn as they had done all day. The largest among them, the leather-clad man, held out his hand, and the mayor passed him the flour sack as the other guards divided to their posts.

The leather-clad man stomped toward the barn, leaving the mayor alone in the snow painted orange with firelight. The mayor seemed to be staring back at Berg through the cracks, and the young giant felt a chill run through him.

The leather-clad man slid beneath the canvas drape, then threw the sack of food to the dry-dirt floor. He glanced to the right, finding Berg pressed against the wall of the barn.

"Stay here. Eat your food, giant. The mayor said you aren't allowed to leave anymore."

"But I am the night-watch," Berg said. He wanted everything to go back to being simple, an easy trade, him walking the town for a bit of food and an occasional friendly visitor in the barn.

"Not anymore," the man said as he left Berg to sit with his thoughts and worries on his own.

PAINT ON IRON

Berg stirred, lost and alone, hopelessly searching the cracks in the ceiling of the barn for watchful-moon. The food the leather-clad man had given him was unsettling, a collection of kitchen scraps and burned bread. He'd eaten worse, but not since he'd arrived at Eisenstadt.

It was full-dark and silent. Berg tried to look through the cracks at the fire, but not even a ribbon of smoke remained. He wasn't sure he trusted his eyes because as he looked at the guards, he noticed a sprinkling of blue sparkles dancing around each of their heads. As they slept in the cold night air, the snow continued to fall, burying them and the valley beneath a velvet veil.

Berg saw him then, standing outside the circle of sleeping guards. Ünhold. He waited in the snow, as still as timber. Hot breath seeped from his nose, leaving behind thick clouds that lingered before they floated to the sky to join the storm.

As Berg watched, the old one walked toward the barn. Berg heard the rough rustle of the canvas flap, and he held his breath as Ünhold wormed his way in through the jagged hole. He could not stand fully in the barn, so he crawled on his knees toward Berg. He reached inside the satchel and pulled out a long silver key.

Berg had seen the key before, but the last time it looked as long as the mayor's arm. Tonight it seemed no larger than a cactus needle as Ünhold held it between his thumb and finger. The old one stared at the young giant, and Berg held out his hands.

With the iron bindings once again lying in the dust, Ünhold turned and took a few steps toward the door. He looked over his shoulder, and Berg knew the ancient one expected him to follow.

At first Berg was too concerned with following the old giant to notice that the town had changed. But it was impossible to ignore the red and yellow flags that hung from long ropes stretched across the street. Ünhold ducked beneath the first of them, then plodded on, bobbing down to slide beneath more flags and ropes as he worked his way toward the heart of Eisenstadt. The carts and wagons that had poured into town lined the streets on either side. Tan canvas had been stretched across hooped beams, converting the wagons into makeshift shelters for the sleeping visitors.

The giants trudged through the city, one behind the other, until Ünhold stopped at the far wall. A near-dawn sun gifted an ounce of light to the world, taking an edge off the dark as Berg joined him.

The old giant lowered a gnarled finger, as warty and wide as an oak branch, and pointed to a painting on the city wall. Berg knelt, feeling the cold caress of snow against one knee, and studied the image.

The design was crude, scribbled quickly on the iron surface with broad strokes of bright-colored paint. The painting was new, yet the image was familiar to Berg. A giant growled on the wall, his open mouth full of sharp teeth as white as bone. Horns protruded from wild hair, and his eyes were full of hate and fire. Around him, an army threatened the beast with biting-ropes and pointed-sticks and torches topped with flames.

Berg placed his hand against the painting. The paint was frozen, but not dry, and as his hand heated the paint, it smeared off, sticking to his skin like colored tar.

His chest compressed with fear, and he began to pant, filling the air with huffs of worried breath. He stood and looked at the ancient giant face to face.

"Do you know what this is?"

Ünhold stared back but held his voice.

"Why won't you talk to me? Who did this? Why did you bring me here?"

All of Berg's questions were left unanswered.

Berg raised his voice. "Don't you know who this is?" He pointed to the giant on the wall, its crude outline snarling.

The ancient one stood quiet, staring at Berg in the near-dawn.

"It's you, you fool," Berg said in full voice, not caring who might hear or if they would come. "It's you. Ünhold. The monster. They are coming for you. You must leave. Do you understand anything I say?"

Ünhold held up his hand. It hung between them like a barricade, halting Berg's outburst. The old giant curled his hand to a fist, leaving his longest finger stretched out, pointing at Berg. He pressed the finger against the young giant's chest. His touch was light, yet the feel of it made Berg shiver. Ünhold moved his finger from Berg and placed it on the chest of the giant on the wall.

Berg understood what he was trying to say, but he knew Ünhold was wrong. He had lived among the people. He'd eaten their food. He'd been their protector. The people of Eisenstadt had wrongly injured and bound him before the mayor had showed him kindness, but he couldn't remember them hurting him since.

He thought of Anya's warning words, how she encouraged him to run away. Even she didn't understand that living alone had costs as well. For Berg, sorrow and solitude were far worse than what he had to endure while living in the iron-city. Even if their rules were odd and their demands were high, at least the people of Eisenstadt had allowed him to stay. And they were building him a home. Berg wondered why Ünhold and Anya couldn't see this, and he slumped his shoulders in resignation, knowing there was nothing he could do to convince his little friend or the old giant.

"It is not me they want," he said to Ünhold, his voice as calm and deep as a snowdrift. "It is you."

Ünhold held his gaze, then looked to the top of the iron wall. He looked back at Berg as if to ask him again to follow.

"I'm sorry," Berg said as he shook his head.

Ünhold reached high and found a seam in the iron. He pulled hard, his ancient joints complaining against the cold. He scaled the wall, proving to Berg how foolish and worthless an iron wall was to the giant, then he jumped to the ground on the other side with a *whoomp*. Berg listened as Ünhold walked toward the deep-wild-woods, his wide feet packing the snow with each step.

The sun was lending red to the sky, the color of summer cardinals. Berg turned to go back to his barn, only to see the gangly figure of the mayor sitting astride his alabaster mule. Berg lumbered over to the little man, whose black coat and hat were a stark contrast to the snow-frosted city around them.

"He's gone, and he won't be back," Berg said.

The mayor nodded. "Come, Berg Wenig. We must get you out of the light before the others wake."

"I can go on my own. I can find the barn and let myself in."

"We are not going to the barn. Follow me."

The hooves of the mule were subdued in the snow, but the mayor led him away at a quick pace. A flicker of white caught Berg's eye: a streak of paint caught on the mayor's long, dark cloak. A drip frozen, but, Berg knew, a drip not yet dried.

BOOK SEVEN

WHERE WE LEARN
OF CAGES AND CROWDS

THE TENT

The young giant stood inside the new tent, surrounded by its warmth. Yellow and red wedges of cloth met at the top of the center mast pole, standing proud in the middle of the colossal structure. Berg had never seen anything so grand, so huge. Rock-lined firepits blazed, spread equally around the tent, and fire holes were cut in the canvas to allow smoke to escape and the twinkling of stars to enter.

A black curtain was drawn over the skeletal structure the iron workers had been devoted to for weeks, ever since Berg left to gather Tallest-Tree. Below the curtain a wooden stage extended, as still and polished as a mountain lake.

The tent buzzed with hardworking townsfolk doing odd tasks and adding details to the nearly finished structure. It was magnificent, a true work of craftsmanship and art. As Berg looked at the glorious space, he knew it was too good to be true.

"This is not for me," he said to the mayor standing below him. "I am no fool."

"Well, of course you are not a fool, Berg Wenig, but this tent is for you."

The mayor led him toward the stage. As they walked, guards with biting-ropes drew near. Berg felt his chest constrict, and Anya's warnings rang through his mind again.

The mayor interrupted his thoughts. "Let me explain." He paused for effect, letting the mystery and grandeur of the tent surround them. "Tomorrow, my friend, will be a great day for you. After the sun has set and our visitors have spent their pocket change filling their bellies with the food found in the fine shops of Eisenstadt, we will introduce you to them. Introduce you to the world." He held out his hand and painted a broad smile beneath his waxed mustache to punctuate his words.

Berg listened to the mayor while the five guards around them became ten, then fifteen, then more than he could count.

As he stood in the beautiful tent, the air filled with the scent of oily fire and his heart filled with dread. He had not asked for this. Berg had always wanted to be with other people, to be accepted, but he had not asked to be shown to the world.

"Tomorrow, this cathedral of canvas and iron will be filled with people who have come to see a show. And a show we shall give them, you and I. Our friends, the townsfolk, have worked very hard to prepare this place, as well as to prepare acts of entertainment and delight. The audience will be thrilled to witness our talented citizens, but they have not traveled for days through the ice and snow to see acrobats and sword swallowers. They are here to see the giant. They are here to see you, Berg Wenig."

The mayor stopped in front of the stage, and the flickering firelight cast dancing shadows across his bony face. He looked sincere, grateful even, as he finished up his practiced speech. "That is why this is your house. Because we could not have done any of this without you. You have brought these people here, and they will line our pockets with gold and chant our names with honor wherever they go. But it is you they've come to see. We are forever in your debt, my large friend.

"I have brought you here, built you this, to ask you to do one more task for me. It should be simple, really." The mayor stood even straighter than his normal stance and looked Berg in the eyes. "I need you to be the star of our show, a fierce and dangerous giant. We need you to become a legend. The Giant of Eisenstadt."

Berg wasn't fierce. Berg wasn't dangerous. He didn't want to be thought of in that way. "I don't want to become a legend."

"But Berg Wenig, you are a legend already." The mayor leaned back and gestured to all of the young giant. "Just look at yourself. You've grown six feet since we trapped you like a runaway pet in the center of town."

The army of guards snickered, mocking Berg for being captured so easily. "One day you'll be bigger than the other giant, Ünhold. Do you think you can continue to hide among the trees? How long will you be able to trade rocks and broken birds' eggs for nibbles of food?"

Berg was shocked and embarrassed the mayor knew of his old habits. He wondered how long the mayor had known about him. He thought back to the painting on the wooden fence in the sleeping city not long ago. It was nearly identical to the one on the iron wall, and the young giant thought perhaps the mayor had painted them both.

Berg felt the fool for being tricked so easily, and he felt the fool for not listening to Anya and Ünhold.

"Eventually you'll turn to a life of anger and brutality, just as Ünhold has done. It's inevitable. It's survival. You'll learn to scare and fight your way through the land until you find your demise. Nobody can escape who they are, Berg, and whether you like it or not, you are a giant."

Berg paid close attention to what the mayor was saying, searching hard for what was truth and what were lies hidden within his clever words.

It was true he was a giant, that was obvious, but it was not true that Ünhold had turned to a life of violence to earn his supper. The mayor knew so much about what he saw, but he knew nothing about the secrets that the giants shared. Berg had wondered about some of the ancient giant's habits, but he'd learned that Ünhold was both a taking and a giving giant. He knew Ünhold had filled his cave of treasures by offering trade for the star-blue-sand. He'd learned that Ünhold was not a beast.

And the more he learned of the mayor and the people of Eisenstadt, the more he wondered if the legends of Ünhold were lies as well.

Berg wanted to tell the mayor he was wrong, but he knew it would be of no use. The mayor would not understand because he chose not to. For the mayor was a man of the world, a man of the people. Not a man who could believe in dream-sand and watchful-moons and kindhearted giants.

The guards multiplied in number, and Berg wondered if it was too late to take Anya's advice and run.

The mayor called for a black curtain to be drawn, and three men tugged on a rope wrapped around a high-hung pulley. A dark shroud parted. Berg drew a breath.

"This is your new home, Berg Wenig," the mayor said as the curtains swung to a stop at either side of the cage.

What Berg saw terrified him. The cage was imposing with its sharp angles and bars as wide as tree trunks. The mayor had built this awful trap, and Berg knew the man would stop at nothing to place a giant behind its iron bars.

"So, my friend. Our giant friend. Will you enter your glorious home and wait for us to part the curtains again? And when we do, will you give the people a show they won't forget?"

Berg was not a beast, and he knew he could never be one for the mayor or for the small men of Eisenstadt. He began to back away as he shook his massive head. "No. I will not. I am not a beast."

The mood in the tent shifted, and the guards began to uncoil the biting-ropes from their shoulders.

"But Berg Wenig," the mayor said, "these men have built you a castle. A finer display of metalcrafting has never existed. Don't dishonor their deeds, Berg Wenig. It would not be kind. It would not be good."

Berg shook his head again as the men dangled the metal teeth of the ropes at their sides. "I can't. I want to leave. I am not your monster."

The mayor raised the first two fingers on his right hand, and the white paint on his cuff caught Berg's eye. A wave of ropes shot through the air before Berg could duck away. A painful web of copper hooks and hemp rope buried the giant.

For the first time in his life, Berg fought back, pulling the men from their feet like rag dolls. He heaved forward, one tortured step at a time toward the entrance of the tent, dragging the army of guards along as they struggled to hold on to their ropes. Commands flew from the mayor's mouth, but the young giant paid them no mind as he labored onward. More men rushed toward the fight, slinging ropes and jabbing at Berg's thighs and shins with long wooden sticks capped with shiny metal ends.

Twelve men on horseback burst through the tent flap, swinging weighted ropes at their side. The added strength of the cavalry overcame the giant, crushing his spirit as he was once again pulled to the earth.

The men howled like a pack of wolves as they brought the giant down with a crash that thundered inside the tent.

THE CAGE

The guards must have planned on it being difficult to convince Berg because they had designed the iron-cage with that in mind. The biting-ropes they used to capture him fit perfectly through massive pulleys bolted to the back of the cage, and they hooked the ropes to teams of mules and horses to drag the battered giant inside his prison.

The bleeding had stopped, but Berg's body was covered with rips and scratches and fresh wounds that felt hot. The fires in the tent had died away, leaving him in the dark. He sat inside the cage and looked through the holes in the canvas above him. He could see a thousand-thousand stars. There would be no snow that night.

Berg wanted to leave, but he knew that was a fool's dream now. He also knew beyond any doubt that he would not rise and shout and carry on for the people. He would not be the mayor's show dog. He would not bark. When the curtains opened, he would sit in the cage and stare at his feet and nothing more. Berg would not feed their false legends and give them lies to fuel the nightmares of children.

He heard the striking of a match and watched two small hands light a pale candle in the center of a ceramic dish. He recognized Anya as she held the candle as high as she could, inspecting the wounded giant in the dark cage.

"They hurt you."

"Yes."

"You tried to leave."

"Yes."

"They made you stay."

"Yes."

They listened to the night and watched the candle begin to melt, leaving a puddle of wax on the polished floor of Berg's cage.

"I had a dream, Berg. One I wanted to share with you, because you were in it," Anya said in the near-dark.

Berg listened, but he had no response. Dreams meant nothing to him now.

"It was a good dream. In it, you were walking through a city, delivering dreams to restless people. You brought them hope and peace and love, and, in return, the people gave you offerings of food and clothing and riches." She paused, watching the hypnotic flame. "It was so real. It felt true."

"You have your giants confused. It is not me who delivers dreams. It's Ünhold, and now he's gone away," Berg said with a voice of defeat.

"But that's just it—it wasn't him. In the dream *you* were the dream-giant. I know because you carried me on your shoulder as you went about your dream-giving task. You even let me help, passing me a handful of dream-sand to pour on the windowsill of a sleeping home. It was the most beautiful thing I've ever seen. The sand pile spun around, and then it floated in and entered the home like a spirit. Like a ghost."

"This dream can never be true. At one time, perhaps, but now I am his. I am only this. I belong to the mayor."

A guard hollered. The light of a torch spilled from behind the black curtain. Anya spoke quickly.

"The dream gave me hope, Berg." She looked to her left and saw two guards hurrying toward them. She pulled out a white-and-red-striped bag and set it down next to the candle. "This is not the end of your story. Goodbye, Shorty."

She zipped away into the dark before the guards arrived. The two burly men found the candle and the bag inside the cage and snapped them up before Berg thought to hide them away.

"What's this?" one asked the other as he opened the bag.

"It looks like he's got himself a little friend," the other said, his smile looking evil in the flickering torchlight. "And I saw who it was. It was the mayor's sneaky niece. I recognize that awful orange hair even in the dark."

"The mayor will be happy to know this," said the first. He stuck a lemon drop in his mouth.

"Don't eat them all," the other said as he slapped the first on the back of his head.

Berg slumped on the floor and lay on his back as he listened to the guards walk away, fighting over the bag of sweets and who would tell the mayor what they had found. He looked into the sky at the stars, then closed his eyes.

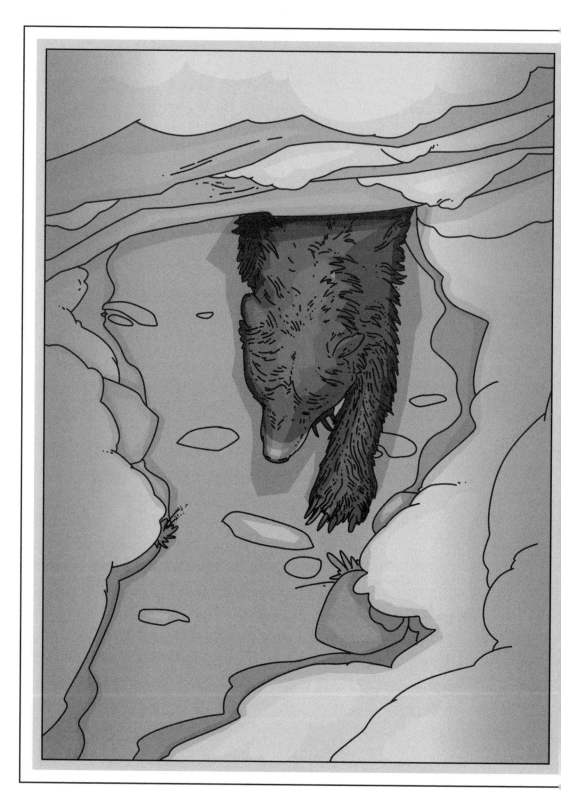

THE SHOW

Berg hunkered in his cage all day, barely moving, the cool bars pressing furrows into his back. Guards had stuffed food and drink inside the cage with him. It sat spoiling. Untouched. Ignored. Refused.

The tent was silent while the sun was high, but it came to life as the sky turned black. The crowd filled the tent like water released from a dam, and Berg listened nervously as their frenzied voices roared. The firepits and torches were lit. Their amber glow caused sweat to pour from Berg, stinging the cuts and scrapes that marked his body.

The people of Eisenstadt entertained the rowdy crowd, and the young giant tried to ignore the energy in the tent. But when a chorus of brass horns belched, he stood and extended his fingers between the iron bars and peeked between the black curtains to see what was happening.

The crowd, an energized collection of old and young and everything in between, cheered and waved their arms at what they saw on stage. They were packed in tight, even holding one another on their shoulders, stacking in two deep to see the giant.

Waves of sadness merged with horror as Berg felt the crowd's growing anticipation of seeing the beast they'd been promised. He had tried his strength against the blue-iron before. He had tried to break his chains earlier, and his hands bore the marks where the cuffs had gouged into his flesh. The chains were nothing compared to the strength of the iron cage. But it wasn't the cage that made him feel trapped. It was the realization that he had become the mayor's toy. His plaything. He was being used by someone who once called him a friend, and that hurt more than any biting-ropes ever could.

The crowd hollered their approval as a troupe of acrobats left the stage, then hushed as the ringmaster walked on, his solitary presence and confident manner drawing their attention in tight.

The mayor had shed his black and gray clothing for something decidedly more fitting for his role as commander of the crowd. A purple coat with long split tails covered a white shirt and black pants of velvet with a matching purple stripe down each leg. His slender build was extended by a top hat, and on his pointed feet, he wore black shoes so shiny they looked as if they had been dipped in oil. He waited quietly for the crowd to give him their complete attention.

When the mood was set, he told his story while resting his white-gloved hands upon a cane topped with the grinning head of a blue-iron wolf.

"Ladies and gentlemen. Children of all ages. Visitors from far-off lands. Dancers and actors and magicians have delighted us tonight. Acrobats and sword swallowers have thrilled us with their talents and bravery. We've laughed along with painted clowns and marveled at the skillful hands of jugglers, but tonight I present you with something more rare and dangerous than anything you have seen before."

The crowd clung to every word from the mayor's mouth, and Berg found himself interested against his will in what the mayor would say next.

"Like you, I was raised on the legends of giants. Brutal beasts that roamed the hills and mountaintops and hid within the dark spaces beneath bridges and shaded forests. There were times when I believed the legends, and times when I thought them to be nothing more than myths buried beneath a thick coat of imagination. But recently something changed all of that for me. And, unbeknownst to you, it changed for you as well."

The mayor removed his gloves, tucking them slowly into the chest pockets of his purple coat.

"Two years ago, I began to hear the awful stories of a mountain giant. Not the legends of our forefathers, but new stories, telling of impossible feats and devastating acts. Tales of a beast that demolished entire towns with his fists of stone. I heard rumors of him stealing children to cook over fires in his mountain cave. I sent a team of hunters to capture him, only to discover that my men had been eaten by the savage beast himself."

The mayor paused to listen to the oohs and aahs of the crowd.

"I decided to let the legend die. It was too dangerous a quest, and one far too risky to further gamble the lives of my men. Then, one day, I received a letter. A fine drawing showed the back of the giant as he walked away from a smoldering village at the base of the Bohleese Mountains. The humble homes of a broken people were leveled to the ground. Fires followed in the giant's wake. A young boy cried as he stood alone, left in this cold world to fight for himself. I turned the drawing over and written across its back were two words I could not ignore."

The mayor paused again as the crowd held its breath and leaned in.

"Help us," the mayor said.

The crowd exhaled as one, struck by the simple plea the master storyteller shared.

Berg let the curtain close and covered his ears. He'd heard enough of the mayor's lies about him, but the forceful tenor of the man's voice carried his words to him against his will.

"This request spoke to my heart, and I knew I must find the brutal giant and rescue those helpless people. It took me and a team of forty men six months to track down the beast. We fought him for thirteen days at the top of a high mountain peak before he relented. And tonight, for the first time ever, I present to you the Giant of Eisenstadt."

The mayor signaled with a bare hand, and the black curtain parted like an opening book.

Exposed, Berg blinked as light from the tent rushed him. The crowd gasped, their voices dwarfed by the enormity of the boy-giant locked behind the ornate cage of blue-iron. Berg tasted terror bubbling up from his stomach, but he stood as still as stone and thought about what the mayor wanted him to do. He wanted him to roar. To frighten the people. To show them what a beast he could be, but the young giant had another idea.

Berg lifted his eyes and pushed his round cheeks up with the corners of his magnificent mouth. He smiled so wide and cheerful that his ears rose a few inches. The people were confused by the smiling giant, and he closed his eyes and pictured Anya smiling in the loft of his barn and the sunshiny taste of lemon-drop candies. He was pleased with his decision to grin at the people, and as he heard the crowd respond, he felt the smile glowing on his face.

One man near the stage asked the mayor if they had caught him by offering him a giant-sized cake. A young woman shouted that he was cute and claimed loudly that the giant was nothing but an oversized baby. Others laughed nearby, and Berg felt a giggle rise up from deep inside him.

He was listening to the crowd, basking in his act of smiling defiance, when he heard the nasal voice of the mayor shouting at him. His top hat was askew, and he waved his wolf-head cane toward Berg as if it were a threat. The giant leaned down to hear the words of the angry little man.

"You give me what I want, or you will force me to do something we will both regret," the mayor shouted.

"Will you poke me with your tiny stick?" Berg asked as he continued to smile.

"I can't hurt you, giant." He spat out the word *giant* as if it burned inside his mouth. "But I can hurt your sneaky friend."

The mayor pointed toward the crowd with his wolf-head cane, and Berg saw Anya standing in the front of the people, pressed up against the stage. Her bright hair was an array of knots and snarls. Her eyelids were puffy, and the tip of her nose was red from crying.

The leather-clad man stood behind her, his face stern and void of emotion as he waited for instructions from the mayor. As Berg watched, the leather-clad man draped the copper hook of a biting-rope over Anya's shoulder, and the hint of a smile cracked across his face.

Hot anger seared Berg from inside. He stood, his head pressing against the top of the cage. The crowd lost its playful banter as they felt hatred drift from the imprisoned giant.

"Let her go!" Berg commanded in a voice meant only for the leather-clad man, but others heard as well.

"That's better, giant," the mayor said. "Now roar for me."

Berg raised his hands and grabbed two of the iron bars. "Let her go now."

The crowd talked nervously, their volume rising and rumbling like an approaching storm.

The mayor laughed his goatlike guffaw. "I'm afraid it's too late for that, giant. You disobeyed me."

The mayor nodded at the leather-clad man, and the man wrapped the biting-rope around Anya's birdlike neck and latched it together with its shiny copper end.

Anya remained very brave, not making a sound, but Berg could read the terror on her face.

Berg roared, sending a wave through the crowd that pleased the mayor and terrified the audience.

The mayor turned to face the crowd again. He straightened his hat with his wolf-head cane, then raised his hands above his head. "My friends, my friends. Have no fear. The mighty warriors of Eisenstadt are not only powerful enough to bring down the giant, Berg Wenig, but they are also masters of metalcraft. The cage is made of our blue-iron, the strongest metal on the face of earth. The cage that holds the beast will contain his strength. I assure you."

The mob stared at Berg inside his prison, and he roared again as the leather-clad man dragged Anya away, stealing her dark eyes from him. Berg smashed his fists against the cage and shouted for the mayor to let her go. The mayor spun to give Berg a quick smile, then returned his attention to the crowd as if Berg's pleas meant nothing to him.

"My friends," he shouted over the angry giant. "Those who have trusted this beast have ended up as bones in his stew. Shout back at him, and he will cower, for he is only a stupid, simple beast."

Berg heard the mayor's instructions. The mayor wanted him to shrink away as the crowd shouted at him, but Berg was overwhelmed with rage. He was desperate to escape and find Anya.

The mob shouted at the giant, their faces curdling red, spittle shooting from their bitter mouths, gnarled veins protruding from their foreheads. Berg took a step back, pressing against the rear of the cage, and the people cheered, misreading his actions for those of a coward.

Berg shot forward, slamming his broad head and muscled shoulder against the front of the cage.

The iron bars bent, and the people screamed. He backed away once more and rammed the cage again. Berg looked at the crowd, searching for Anya, but he couldn't see her red hair anywhere in the sea of people. Panic fueled him as he backed away and smashed the cage a third time. Rivets shot like bullets from the tortured bars, shooting over the crowd and tearing through the walls of the tent.

The crowd shrieked, and Berg watched the mayor, whose voice was swallowed up in the panic of the mob, his arms flapping like a wounded crow as he tried to convince them to stay.

Berg's eyes were clouded, dazed by his forceful ramming. Blood ran from his forehead where a metal bar had lashed at him, and drool dripped from his chin. He roared again, sending a burst of hot air through the tent that rippled the canvas.

The mob divided, rushing and pushing for the edges of the tent, some crawling under the flaps and others cutting through the thin walls with pocket-knives. But a hundred-hundred men stayed behind, determined to protect the others and try their hands against the beast.

Firelight flickered in Berg's eyes as he became the monster they desired. He found the mayor and passed him a glare that robbed the color from the man's skin. The little man stared back in his fancy clothes, true fear shadowing his hollow face.

Berg stepped back again, filled his lungs, and then smashed at the cage again. The cry of bending metal screeched through the tent, and the crowd erupted. The mayor shouted endlessly, furious that nobody was following his orders.

Men rushed to the firepits and burned their hands as they tossed flaming coals and half burned logs upon the stage surrounding Berg. The oiled wood accepted the fire with greed, and the mayor began to back away from the crowd, drawing nearer to Berg in his iron trap.

The mayor shouted to the guards that remained, ordering them to put out the fire, but the terrified guards ran from the burning platform with the mob.

Berg's anger raged, and he heard the shouting of the crowd continue as they fled from the tent. The fire rushed toward him and the mayor, flowing across the stage, a burning river with murderous intent. It climbed the black curtains surrounding the stage with twin columns of fire.

The fire was closing in, and Berg could smell the fear on the mayor as the narrow man backed up against his cage. Flames jumped from the curtains to the roof of the tent. Berg wedged himself between the back of the cage and the bottom of a single bar of blue-iron. He jammed his foot against the bar and pressed with all his might until it curved, opening a gap wide enough for a skinny man to slide through.

"Get in," he shouted to the mayor.

The mayor was unaccustomed to taking orders, and he looked frantic as he searched for an escape of his own design. He began to cough and spit and choke.

"Through the bars. I'll save you," Berg shouted through the smoke.

The mayor, nearly surrounded by fire, looked up at the giant, his eyes full of panic. "No. You'll eat me. You're the beast after all."

"I am not. I am Berg the giant, but I am no beast," Berg pleaded with the man. "Quick. Inside the cage."

Berg saw the mayor's legs wobble, and then he watched the mayor topple to the stage. His top hat rolled into the fire, where it was gobbled up in a flash of sparks and ash.

Berg squeezed his hand through the gap in the cage and reached for the mayor, intending to pull him toward what little safety the cage might offer. But the cowardly mayor mistook Berg's intent, and, filled with a fear irrational and hot, he pushed his way back into the flaming stage, where he shouted until he became nothing more than a memory.

Berg's eyes stung with smoke, and he drew hot air through his teeth as he tried to pry his way out of the cage, struggling for release from his iron trap. The clanging metal and the shouting crowd roared outside the tent. The unmistakable drumming of war.

The walls of the tent tore open to reveal a moon as full and round and un-ashamed as any Berg had ever seen. A shadow rushed through the flames, and the broad head of an ax the size of a horse cart rose to blot out the face of the moon.

Berg cringed as the ax swung toward him. White and orange sparks melted into the fire as the metal tore through the hot blue-iron bars, carving a gash in the cage. The ax rose again, and in the fiery moonlight, Berg saw the white beard of Ünhold. Upon his head, the ancient giant wore a massive crown of branches, looking every bit like the horned beast painted on city walls and whispered about by terrified townsfolk.

The ax fell, and the giant demolished the back wall of the cage with his second swing.

Berg ran from the flaming ruins, Ünhold following close behind. The cold air outside the tent contrasted with the smoke Berg had inhaled, and he and Ünhold hacked and coughed as they ran. They emerged from the flames only to be surrounded by a pack of armed men.

Two biting-ropes dug into Berg's forearm. More ropes flew toward him as Ünhold ran to his side, his beard and tree-branch-horns tossing embers into the sky. The ancient one used the ax to cut the ropes that bound the younger giant, and he nudged Berg away with his shoulder.

Berg tottered then looked at Ünhold as he fought the army. His bare feet were black with soot, and his body was riddled with wounds. Flames covered the crown of horns Ünhold wore upon his head.

Berg had never seen such a magnificent and powerful creature. Ünhold was truly a warrior.

The young giant ran to join him, eager to fight by his side, two terrible giants battling an unfair mob of armed men. More men rushed forward on horseback, swinging biting-ropes and leading with long, iron pointed-sticks.

Berg kicked a group of men away and swam through the fray to fight alongside the enormous giant, but Ünhold turned and pushed him away again, this time with the end of Berg's once-buried ax.

One of the men on horseback drove his iron pointed-stick through the meat of Ünhold's leg, and a hundred-hundred biting-ropes pulled the ancient giant to his knees. Ünhold turned his head of fire and horns toward the young giant and shouted the only word Berg would ever hear him speak.

"Run!"

And while Berg had always been an obedient giant, he refused to run away.

The crowd around the giants turned to chaos. A hundred-hundred men raged in, spurred on by the tumbling of the ancient one. As one, they swung their weapons. But the army of tiny men underestimated their foes as Berg rushed forward to rescue Ünhold.

Using his wide and callused feet, Berg pushed and kicked his way through the crowd. Men and horses were no match for the tenacious giant as he shoved them aside like a child wading through a room of toys.

The leather-clad man shouted to his men, rallying them to focus on Berg, but their biting-ropes had already ensnared Ünhold, so the young giant moved forward with ease.

In his anger, every muscle of his body tensed, and those men who were able to get close to him with their metal pointed-sticks were met with frustration as their weapons failed to find purchase.

A swarm of men buried Ünhold, doing their best to stab and strangle the giant.

Berg yanked them a handful at a time from the giant's back, tossing them to the crowd with reckless abandon. The night was bright orange, and the flames from the burning tent leaped into the sky as Berg raged, digging through the men to reach his target.

While Berg was intent on saving his friend, there was something else on his mind. A hope combined with a dream told to him by a young girl with bright red hair. When Berg reached Ünhold, he grabbed hold of the satchel slung around his battered shoulder. He yanked with all his might, and the leather strap that held the bag in place snapped.

Berg stood, his mother's satchel in his hands. He roared to the crowd with such fury that the horses bolted, ignoring the commands of the men on their backs. As he straightened to his full height, bathed in blue from watchful-moon and painted orange from the angry fire at his back, he was nothing short of magnificent.

His warning roar echoed through the city of iron, and then the giant spun toward the burning cage. He ripped the deer-bone button from the satchel, opened the flap, and, with a mighty throw, launched the bag full of star-blue-sand into the belly of the fire.

As his mother's satchel tumbled through the air, dream-sand spilled from the bag, sprinkling glittery flecks of azure so bright they flashed white against the flames. For a split second, Berg was caught in their enticing dance as the specks began to glow even brighter than the sun.

Then Berg threw himself against the body of Ünhold, covering him from a blast so bright and brilliant it would make a falling star proud.

S!LK

Acrid smoke filled Berg's nostrils as he woke. Ink-black ashes floated down around him like midnight-colored snow as the sun said a morning hello in the other-west. At first, he was unsure where he was; his mind felt full of mud, and his memories seemed a thousand-thousand miles away.

The ground was littered with pointed-sticks and shields and the lifeless bodies of a hundred-hundred biting-ropes. Piles of rock and twisted iron lay in mounds where the buildings nearest to the star-explosion had been leveled to the ground. Nothing was left of the iron cage the mayor had built for Berg but a gnarled and warped mass of black and shimmering blue.

Then he saw her, his brave and bright Anya walking toward him. Her orange hair unfurled and uncovered in the morning sun reminded him of firelight, and an ember of hope began to warm him deep inside.

In her hands she carried an oak bucket wrapped in iron bands, steam rising from the water inside. She arrived at his side, quietly. Somber. Bound to a task she was determined to perform. She placed the bucket at Berg's feet, then pulled a long scarf the color of lemon-drop candies from inside her shawl. She plunged the silken scarf into the bucket of hot water, and then she wrung it out before she began to wash the wounds on Berg's burned and battered feet.

She looked up at him and smiled as she saw he was awake. "Hey, Shorty," she said in a voice as beautiful to Berg's ears as any songbird he'd ever heard. "You sure can sleep."

Berg smiled in return, then looked around.

Standing nearby, huddled in small groups of three and four, the people of Eisenstadt watched the two friends. Berg looked them over, the bowed heads, how they leaned on one another for strength. Occasionally the tiny hand of a child would flicker a quick wave to the giant.

"They are watching us," Berg said in a gravelly voice, his throat as dry as winter wheat.

"Most of the people have gone, but those who stayed behind aren't scared of you anymore. Without the mayor to stoke them with his lies, they are beginning to see you like I do," Anya said as she looked up at Berg.

A tear the size of large strawberry rolled down Berg's cheek and splashed on his burlap tunic, leaving behind a chocolate-colored drop that somehow looked and felt to Berg like gratitude.

As his head began to clear with cleansing thoughts of being understood by the people, Berg remembered Ünhold. He turned to look for the ancient giant, and he saw him lying upon the ground, his face still and cold, pressed against soot-covered cobblestones.

Berg rolled over to stand, but Anya placed her hand against him, her touch as light as a feather, warning him. Berg paused and looked down at her in the street.

She shook her head, and Berg's worries were confirmed as another strawberry-sized tear found its way to the burned dirt between his feet.

"He is gone, my friend," Anya said. "I'm sorry."

Slowly, Berg crawled to the quiet giant. He brushed a white lock of hair from Ünhold's face, its matted end singed black by the fires of the night before. He pressed his wide palm against the shoulder of the giant he barely knew.

As he thought of the people watching him in the center of the burned city of iron, he wished more than anything that the ancient giant could have seen them like this. Patient. Understanding. Peaceful. Berg knew their new kindness wasn't just for him—it was for Ünhold as well, and the hurt of knowing the old one would never know it was nearly more than Berg could bear.

He rolled the giant over, then reached beneath his square head and tree-trunk legs and stood with Ünhold in his arms.

The ancient one was heavy, but Berg found a new strength within himself that felt endless. He looked toward the mountain peak, toward the fallen star and the cave of Ünhold.

"I have a task to do. It will not be easy."

Anya stood by his side, looking up toward the cave as well. "The most important things are not."

"Goodbye, Anya."

"Goodbye, Shorty."

As winter took her place on the earth, sharing the first flakes of what would become a deep and healing storm, Berg took a step toward Ünhold's cave. He was as sad as he'd ever felt in a thousand-thousand days, but somehow, that sadness seemed to fit in all the right spots for once. It was all around him, but it didn't crush him as it had done in the past. It was centered firmly in his heart in a place where the giant recognized it for what it was. In a place the giant could manage.

THE CAVE

The giant stood next to the star embedded in the floor of his cave. The walls curved upward in a mellow slope as warm and inviting as a womb. The air around him smelled of dry meats and raw onions, and a hint of his new favorite candies lingered in the air. Peppermint—the taste of cold, wintery wind.

A spring shower let itself into the cave, small drops of diamonds pattering as they landed upon the fallen star like tears. Berg wiped the moisture away, feeling a power within the star-stone that was much older and wiser than he could understand. Watchful-moon spied on him through the hole in the roof of the cave, and then a cloud moved aside and a blue-white moonbeam tiptoed further into his home. Berg followed her light, wondering, not for the first time, if the moon shined just for him.

As if in reply, the moonlight rested on the surface of a leather satchel. It was crudely made, but it still hinted at memories of the two giants who had gone before Berg. Two giants who had once taken up the mantle he now wore.

A new and vibrant thread of bright red was wound around a deer-bone button, and Berg knelt to pick up the satchel in his wide hands.

He thought of his mother, tucking him away in the safety of a hole so that his story could continue, even if it meant hers could not.

He thought of Ünhold, his ancient body filled with strength as he gave his life to save Berg's.

The debt he owed them was monumental, but it was a debt he intended to repay.

He placed the bag reverently over his shoulder, then tucked his sad feelings into their place within his heart and stepped out into the rain. The little spring drencher was warm and inviting, and as he made his way toward the city in the moonlight, he passed a mound of earth so large and round that men would someday mistake it for a mountain.

Berg reached inside the satchel, burying his wide fingers in the dream-sand, and pulled out a handful of glittering particles. As he passed the mound, he sprinkled it with star-blue-sand and smiled.

"I am on my way, old friend," Berg said to the mound of earth. "I have a great deal to do. It won't be easy, but as a friend once told me, the most important things are not."

Berg watched as the dream-sand landed on the mound of earth, its surface covered with budding spring flowers and fresh, tender grass. It seemed to glow in the moonlight, a sparkling tribute Berg hoped he'd be able to capture in his mind's eye as he went on his journey.

The snorting of a horse caught Berg's attention, and he looked to the west. Anya sat brave and bright on the back of a proud tawny horse, her hair so orange its color defied the night.

"Come on, Shorty. We have dreams to share," Anya said to the Dream-Giant. Then she nudged her horse toward the deep-wild-woods, and Berg took chase with his heart full of hope and his satchel full of star-blue-sand.

ACKNOWLEDGMENTS

Without him, this book would have been a shadow of itself—my brainstormer, my deep thinker, my best friend, Tanner.

Without her, this book would have lacked heart—Brynn's determination to find herself while surrounded by wolves showed me it takes love, not anger, to grow.

Without her, this book would have lacked courage—Malorie is a fighter with an artist's eye, a warrior with the courage of a lion, a fearless pioneer who knows exactly who she is.

Without her, this book would have lacked beauty—Annie's attention to the small things and her love for all things bright and beautiful were my North Star when things in Berg's life became nearly too much to bear.

Without her, this book would not be in your hands—Pam believed and fought long after other believers and fighters had given up. My friend, my confidant, my ever-patient traveler. Our journey has just begun.

Without them, this book would be a hundred-hundred loose ideas and a thousand-thousand unclear thoughts—Chris and Lisa were not just guides; they became friends and reminded me of something I had lost along the way. Story matters most.

But most of all, without her, I would not be an artist. She is my Watchful-Moon, shining bright. Full and round and unashamed. Slowly guiding with love, supporting with strength, and believing with passion beyond measure. The word *muse* is not nearly enough—Jodi, you are my everything.